D1083269

by

Corbett Davis Jr.

Artwork

by

Andy Marlette

MINDSTIR MEDIA

"Corbett has always been one of the best fly fisherman I have known and now his abilities to spin a mystery yarn are catching up with his perfection at fly casting."

- Jimmy Buffett

"Until now I only knew Dead Man's Fingers as the part of a crab that was not edible. Corbett Davis has given the name a whole new meaning in an authentic salty setting with some truly weird characters in this spellbinding novel."

- Jimbo Meador

"Dead Man's Fingers is the stuff of Florida dreams: Booze and seafood. Heat and hangovers. Secret offshore jaunts to Cuba and jet ski cremation services. Elaborate financial crimes and obligatory Viagra jokes. And throughout all of it, there's plenty of good fishing, of course. Corbett Davis Jr. casts a line from the waters of Pensacola to the flats of the Florida Keys, and you never know what he's going to reel in on the next page -- especially when it's evidence of murder. Happy fishin'."

- Andy Marlette, Pensacola News Journal Political Cartoonist

"He who is not contented with what he has,
would not be contented with what he would like to have."
-Socrates

"Earth provides enough to satisfy every man's needs,
but not every man's greed."
-Mahatma Gandhi

"Get Greedy, Become Needy."
-Abraham Levin

Published by Mindstir Media LLC
45 Lafayette Rd. Suite 181 | North Hampton, NH 03862 | USA
1.800.767.0531 | www.mindstirmedia.com

Printed in the United States of America
ISBN-13: 978-0-9993872-9-0
Library of Congress Control Number: 2017914687

Books by Corbett Davis, Jr.

Fiction

Dead Man's Fingers
Dead Low
The Deadly Reef

Contributing Author

West of Key West

Dedication

To the less than civilized group of fly-fisherman, comprised of rock stars, doctors, dentists, authors, artists, restaurateurs, French Counts, pilots, boat captains, tour guides and one jeweler who gather each year on some exotic tropical island to chase bonefish, solve world problems and sample a variety of alcoholic beverages.

Acknowledgements and Comments

By the author

Although very real places, I use towns like Gulf Breeze, Pensacola, Cudjoe Key and Key West in the most fictional sense of my imagination. You may recognize some of the local dives, restaurants, and locations, but "Dead Man's Fingers" is a fabricated story. With the exception of Captain Rush Maltz and Charlie Switzer, all of the characters mentioned are products of the author's warped imagination.

Captain Rush Maltz is an offshore fishing guide in Key West, whom I have spent many great moments with on the ocean. Together we have shared plenty of adventures and caught more fish than we deserve. Rush is a native (conch) Key Wester and lives in the lower Keys with his wife, Kelley, and their two children Kade and Kora.

Charlie Switzer is also a very real person living in Pensacola with his wife Fran. Charlie is a good friend whom I have known since high school. Although a character in his own right, the only thing he shares with Sir Charles Switzer in the book is his lovable, quirky personality and his name. Again, all else is strictly fiction, especially the murder and sex. And I hope he and his wife will still speak to me after this printing.

Powell, Dawn, Limbo, and I want to thank our friends for helping us through yet another adventure.

First, I would like to thank my loving wife, DeeDee, for her inspiration and motivation throughout the writing of this book. Without her constantly standing by my side, her school teacher attention to detail and her undeniable editing abilities, I would have had this written a year ago. But it most likely would not have been grammatically correct or nearly as readable.

Thanks to my dad who passed on to me his most prized gene, his love of the ocean, family and the Florida Keys.

For Connie Lancaster at Jewelers Trade Shop in Pensacola Florida, much thanks for your dedication and impossible task of translating my scribbled hieroglyphics into a beautifully typed and legible manuscript.

There are plenty of others who have helped me in many different ways to complete this novel. Always carrying a pen and notepad I scribe ideas, thoughts and possible scenes wherever I feel inspired. Most of these places appear in the book, but the people behind them most often do not.

Thanks go to Waldo, Alexis and Felix in Havana, Cuba for introducing me to their country. If not for them I would not know the pleasure of sipping a mojito on the back lawn of Hotel Nationale overlooking the Malecon, or following Hemmingway's tracks to his favorite haunts. I would not have enjoyed fabulous Cuban cuisine with their family and friends. And I'm sure I would never have appreciated the great flavor of Cuban cigars and rum while enjoying the festive show at the Tropicana. Because of these experiences I was able to come to understand their country and their traditions. The love I have for Cuba and the Cuban people inspired me to write about those unique and mysterious places before they became well known to the rest of America.

In the lower Keys: Thanks to Berk and Colleen at KOA Sugarloaf Marina for your kindness and friendship over the years and for your spectacular coconut art. For Captain Rush Maltz with Odyssea Charters out of Murray's Marine who makes every fishing trip an adventure.

Many people who own and operate the bars and restaurants provided a back drop and an array of Keys characters fit for a novel. Lynn at the Square Grouper Bar and Grill on Cudjoe Key, Bobby at Geiger Key Marina, Hogfish Grill and Roostica Pizzeria on Big Coppit Key and Stock Island, Olga and Gary at Baby's Coffee at mile marker 15 in the lower Keys, the Five Brothers in Key West and Ramrod Key, No Name Pub on Big Pine Key and El Sibonay Cuban in Key West are just a few of my favorites.

Finally, back in Gulf Breeze Florida, I would like to thank Corbett III, Sarah, Corbett IV, and Mia along with my wife DeeDee, for making my life a "Happily Ever After" novel itself.

- Corbett Davis, Jr.

Mile Marker 22.8
Cudjoe Key, Florida

PROLOGUE

It was in early summer of 1996 when Powell Taylor's love of salty waters emerged. He was ten the year his dad, Charles P. Taylor, Sr. moved his family to Pensacola Bay in Gulf Breeze, Florida. As a fifth grader, Powell had already learned more about life than most of the prepubescent kids his age. He was lucky enough to grow up in a close family where hard work, respect, honesty, and love were learned through the example his parents lived.

Powell was at that awkward age before little girls caught his eye, but when his dad brought home that first old fiberglass skiff with a ten-horse Johnson, his love of the marine environment, Pensacola Bay, and all of the adventures that came with it was immediate.

Besides fishing, exploring and watching shorebirds, one of his favorite activities was actually nothing more than a daily chore. In an effort to teach his son responsibility and discipline, Charles Taylor, Sr., although loving, was quite strict.

Whether in the winter months after school or early in the mornings on summer days, Powell always looked forward to his favorite task. His mom and dad both loved gumbos, chowders, jambalayas, and any dish with blue crab as an ingredient. Sometimes the family would gather at the end of the dock and boil the live crabs, simply picking out the meat and dipping it in butter. But in most cases, the crabs had to be cleaned first. Growing up on the bay Powell followed his father, watching closely and learning everything he could about catching and cleaning crabs. Whenever he had the chance, the boy would follow his old man anywhere and everywhere.

It was probably these memories with his father that made catching and cleaning crabs one of his favorite pastimes. His father worked hard both day and night building his business in the family jewelry store. So spending time with him on the water was rare but always special. Powell looked forward to his daily duty because he loved it and also because he wanted to make his dad proud.

Three crab traps with a six-foot length of rope were spaced evenly and tied to pilings on the two-hundred-foot dock. If Powell had been fishing or had caught mullet in his cast net, he would save the backbones and heads from the fish he filleted for crab bait. His routine every day was the same. He would untie the traps from the pilings and drag them through the shallow water to his boat, which was anchored a few feet away. Next, he would dump all of the crabs into the boat. While the crabs crawled around on the bottom of the skiff, Powell would rebait the traps. On the rare occasion that he had no fish heads, his mom always had a backup in her freezer. Although not quite as good of bait as fish parts, raw chicken backs and necks worked almost as well. After resetting the traps and tying them back to their designated pilings, Powell returned to his boat. A normal nightly catch for the three traps would be between twenty-five and thirty crabs. After many months of practice, Powell could easily finish cleaning an impressive thirty crabs in an hour. He would smile knowing that was only two minutes per crustacean. To him it was not only a chore, but it was also a challenge, and even more importantly, it was fun. He would grab both claws at the same time being very careful not to get pinched. He would twist them off and toss them in the ice chest. Next, with one hand grasping the crab by its legs, he pried off the top shell with the other hand. He flipped it over and removed the bottom apron. Powell leaned over the side of the boat holding the crab tightly and skimmed it across the water's surface. The pressure from the water forced all of the entrails out. Immediately schools of pinfish showed up to eat the tasty discards. Using his thumb and forefinger, he twisted off the mouth parts. The next step he remembered most vividly from the first time his father taught him how to clean a crab.

"Powell make sure you remove all of the crab's spongy gills from both halves. If not, they will make you very sick. That's why they are called dead man's fingers."

It would not be until high school biology class that Powell learned the gray gills were not poisonous but merely tough and indigestible, but he would always remember the trepidation and exaggerated emphasis in his father's voice that day, "Dead Man's Fingers!"

After college when Powell decided to abandon his career in the family jewelry business to move to the Florida Keys, the lessons and knowledge he gained from that childhood boat proved invaluable. But never did he imagine that twenty years after cleaning his first blue crab would he discover a new meaning, a dreadful meaning, for the poisonous spongy gills he so carefully removed.

CHAPTER 1

I could smell the foul odor of low tide from my back porch overlooking Cudjoe Bay. It was not an unfamiliar smell.

In the three short years I've lived here, I have spent much of my time at home on this deck. I can see the American Shoal Tower that stands one hundred and nine feet tall marking the reef just seven miles due south. Built in 1880, it is a reminder of all the ships and vessels that have passed by. I imagine Black Caesar and Jean Lafitte rode these winds on their sailing ships within sight of where my house now stands. And even in darkness, I know the water is low tonight. Despite the oppressive smell of rotting sargassum weed and small crustaceans that usually are covered by high water, fond memories return. Like a familiar scent that lingers on a pillow reminding you of a girl, the aromas unwillingly transported me back to another time. It is not a pleasant thought.

Captain Limbo and I had fished our way through this same tide before with some distinct challenges, though in a different place and a different time. The conversations about trips of our most dark, immoral, and illegal adventures would never surprise me again. There was much about my friend Limbo that caused me worry and many sleepless nights. So naturally, I was more than curious when he called and woke me up this morning before sunup.

"Powell, we need to talk, and it needs to be soon," Limbo said as I tried hard to focus. Although my full name is Charles Powell Taylor Jr., Limbo, like all of my friends, calls me Powell.

"What? Who is this?" I replied, still in the transitional state from being dead asleep to entering wakefulness. I was experiencing either hypnagogia or somnolence, although I never really did understand the difference between the two. But for a brief moment, my threshold of consciousness included weird dreams and hallucinations.

I was comfortably stuck in a state of sleep paralysis until I heard Limbo shout, "Wake up, Powell! I need to talk to you."

Now that he was off the wagon and back to drinking, Limbo was living on a boat in Key West these days. With so many local bars and waterfront taverns, this was a dangerous environment for anyone, especially a recovering alcoholic. But Limbo had changed over the past months. His recent reckless behavior was concerning and unnerving, and totally unlike him.

Although I had definitely noticed Limbo's glaring transformation in the past weeks, I was not overly concerned. I assumed it was, understandably, a result of our failed attempt to save my girlfriend's life late last year. I have been buried with sadness, sorrow, and relentless guilt. Dawn Landry and I had fallen in love a few years ago and planned on a beautiful life together. With some crazy unfortunate circumstances along with extremely bad luck Dawn was kidnapped and killed by body organ thieves in Havana, Cuba who wanted her heart. This all came at a time when Dawn and I had been arguing over something so ridiculous and minute that I cannot even recall the cause. But my guilt and self-loathing will no doubt bother me for the rest of my life. I made bad choices and horrible decisions during that stressful time when Dawn was missing. I am working on my recovery, and hopefully, someday the pain will ease. With the danger involved in her attempted rescue and trying to simply survive myself, I was never able to say goodbye or hold Dawn in my arms or even see her body after her death. Limbo was the one who found Dawn's body while rushing me away from her, and during the imminent danger, he barely saved my life and his own.

I have many questions to ask Limbo about that night but cannot force myself to revisit those horrible memories yet.

Limbo's boat was anchored off Christmas Tree Island just six hundred forty-five yards northwest of downtown Key West. My home on

Cudjoe Bay lies at mile marker 22. Since I had already planned to fish that morning on a patch of reef off Sugarloaf Key, we decided to meet for lunch halfway between us at Geiger Key Marina. Captain Limbo would most likely show up in "Woodrow," his Ford woodie station wagon. It had belonged to his uncle who bought it new in 1950. When Limbo turned sixteen, the car was a gift from his dad's favorite brother. The car's name, Woodrow, came with the gift. It seems his uncle was quite a history buff and thought Woodrow Wilson was the best president the United States had ever elected. And how appropriate that with the mahogany and maple finishes on the side of the wagon, it was referred to as a "Woodie."

At first, Captain Limbo did not share the same love of Woodrow as his oldest living relative did. In high school, it was downright embarrassing to be seen in it. He would often beg his dad to borrow the family Buick for special dates. And when asked about the car's name, he told fellow classmates it was because the first time he saw it, he got an erection. The word soon spread among the students and the car became a chick magnet. The guys were jealous, and the girls joked they wanted a ride on Limbo's woodie. But alas, Woodrow was a sad sight these days. The faded maroon paint looked very pale next to the weathered, sun-bleached mahogany that now probably carried seventy-five coats of marine spray varnish. With no air conditioner, a broken heater, and an outdated radio, Woodrow looked as if it should be on the streets of Havana instead of Key West. But Limbo's initial perception of the car changed, and he was now always proud to drive it, as he would be today.

I showed up in a much less impressive mode of transportation. My seventeen-foot Maverick skiff with a ninety horse Yamaha was also a gift. My dad, Charles Powell Taylor, Sr. surprised me on my college graduation day in Tallahassee, Florida. Although I loved it, I never named it. However, Woodrow would have been a perfect name for my boat.

I anchored my Maverick skiff in fifteen feet of water off Sugarloaf Key. It took less than five minutes for respectable mangrove, yellowtail, and mutton snapper to respond to the call of the chum line with great enthusiasm. Behind the boat was a beautiful sight. Aquarium-like fish joined the snapper in a frenzy as they darted back and forth enjoying this seafood buffet. I caught one gag and two nice black grouper weighing more than twenty pounds each that I immediately released. It was the third Wednesday of March, the first day of the full moon. Back home in Florida's Panhandle, large migratory female sheepshead borrow every rock, jetty, and wreck on the Gulf Coast. While my friends and family in Gulf Breeze are enjoying fresh fried sheepshead, here in Key West, the grouper season was not open for another five weeks. Although it was hard to release such beautiful grouper I had more than enough snapper for three meals.

I tied off the skiff to the dock pilings with a bow line and another rope off the port side of the stern. I could see Woodrow out in the side parking lot, his faded side baking in the strong midday rays from the overhead sun. When I hopped up on the dock of the restaurant, I glanced around for Limbo. Today was one of those perfect Keys days when the winds were calm, the sun was bright, and the water was slick and glassy. Sunburned tourists paddled kayaks and stand-up paddle boards in the canals surrounding the restaurant and Tiki bar. Every picnic table was full, alive with laughter and colorful fishing stories of who caught what and where they had fished. Standing at the end of the bar under the Tiki Hut, a solo guitarist mimicked well-known artists' island songs. He had just finished singing "A Pirate Looks at Forty," an obvious local favorite. But the song he now sang was unfamiliar to me, something about an old blue chair.

Geiger Key Marina is one of my favorite local Keys hangouts and today was a perfect example why. The animated crowd was a pleasant mixture of burnt-skinned, shirtless, tattooed, and bikini-clad locals amidst a few out-of-towners and campers in tacky t-shirts they purchased in Key West. I recognized a few logos that also hung in my own closet thanks to one too many drinks on Duval Street.

Limbo had indeed beat me to the marina. I spotted him at a small table in the far back on the outside deck. He gazed vacantly across the room. His bottle of Landshark beer was more than half empty and judging from the number of dead soldiers lined up on the table, Limbo most obviously had been waiting for some time. As I snaked my way through the picnic tables, I threw out an acknowledging wave in his direction. He nodded back. Before I joined him and could sit down, he slurred, "Powell, where the hell you been?"

I looked at my left wrist before I answered, "I'm right on time Limbo. It's one thirty."

Undoubtedly feeling no pain, Limbo started babbling immediately as we ordered our food. Later I would realize he had tried to drown his sorrow and guilt to help him say what had been on his mind for seven months. I ordered a fried grouper cheek Po-Boy with a cold draft beer. Limbo ordered two more Landsharks in a bottle.

"I'm not sure where to begin, Powell," Limbo cried desperately.

CHAPTER 2

Charlie Switzer sat among the mangrove roots on the north end of Shark Key. Shading himself in the ninety-eight-degree heat and half-submerged in the salty water, he patiently waited as the sun began to set. The vivid reds, pinks, and oranges that followed the sunset were like a Fourth of July fireworks celebration. But Charlie was unable to fully enjoy the mesmerizing disappearance of the day's sun. His mind was elsewhere.

After the huge orange ball melted into the sea and the colorful sky dissipated, the sudden darkness spawned demons in Charlie's soul. Greed is one of the deadliest of all sins. And Charlie's rapacious desire for wealth and expensive toys would most likely be his downfall one day. But for now, even knowing it would eventually derail, he could not stop this runaway train he rode.

Charles A. Switzer grew up on the Gulf Coast in Florida's Panhandle. He graduated from Pensacola Junior College and then from the University of West Florida, where he earned a business degree in marketing. To be successful in marketing, one must have a great imagination along with much passion and a powerful need to succeed. Charlie possessed all of these traits and became a marketing genius. By the time Charlie turned twenty-five, he owned one of the most successful advertising agencies in Northwest Florida. But it was not until his thirtieth birthday that his ingenious style of marketing changed the advertising industry forever and made him a multimillionaire overnight. Charlie was not only great in marketing a product, but he was also a phenomenal businessman.

On March 27, 1998, three days before Charlie's thirtieth birthday, the FDA approved a drug called Viagra for the Pfizer Pharmaceutical Corporation. The unknown blue pill was a modern medical breakthrough to cure the dreaded impotence in men. The problem was that the only way men knew about Viagra was from their doctor if they had a problem. And the majority of men who did indeed suffer from impotence were not about to discuss it with their doctor or anyone else. They were not only too embarrassed, but they were also devastated by the fact that their penis no longer worked. These men felt that women would laugh at them and ridicule them among their friends. This perception in men's minds made it difficult for Pfizer to address the issue, much less be able to market their new revolutionary wonder drug profitably.

For his birthday, Sir Charles, as he became known in most affluent advertising circles, decided to fly to Key West for a fishing trip with some friends. He landed in Miami and during a three-hour layover, he bought a *Wall Street Journal* and sat at a Cuban-style bar ordering mojitos in every flavor. He was not sure if it was the rum or a sugar high that began to cloud his thoughts. Charlie's eyelids were getting heavy when a particular article in the paper caught his eye. The more he read, the more he sobered up. Finally, he was wide-eyed, wired, and totally focused. The second page headline of the *Wall Street Journal* on March 28, 1998, read as follows:

Unknown Miracle Drug Approved Yesterday by FDA.

The reporter for the *Journal* had written an informative article detailing the new drug called Viagra from Pfizer Pharmaceutical. He explained how it was a cure for impotence in older men but that the cost of research and development was in the millions of dollars. The problem was how exactly to market a pill that could make an impotent man's penis erect.

All of a sudden, it was as if confused seas sloshed around inside of Charlie's skull consuming the fragile lobes of his brain. The thoughts were bouncing around inside his head like a ping pong ball at a bingo parlor. Charlie read further to discover that the FDA had made sure that in any advertising Pfizer had to list all of the warnings and precautions that come with taking the pill. It seemed that the long list of problematic warnings was hindering sales.

Charlie paid his bar tab, then ran to the ticket agent and asked when the next flight to Pensacola departed. Thirty minutes later he was sitting in first class headed north and back home to Pensacola. He made notes and jotted down his ideas while Google gave him all of the phone numbers and contact names he needed at Pfizer Pharmaceutical. Sir Charles was up all night writing his masterful marketing plan. It took three hours of persistence and transfers to seven different extensions before Charlie was able to secure an appointment. When Charlie Switzer put his mind to something, he could be very convincing. Richard Long, the head of marketing for Pfizer Drugs offered to meet Charlie in the New York office at two o'clock the following day.

By the time Charlie arrived at the corporate offices on 42nd Street, he was more than well-prepared. His last twenty-four hours of research were invaluable in his presentation. Charlie had studied not only the Pfizer Corporation but knew everything ever written on this new miracle drug called Viagra. He also knew to the penny the research and development costs for Pfizer to develop the drug.

When Mr. Long entered the room, Charlie's marketing mind kicked in, causing a devious grin on his face that he tried to stifle. But he couldn't help the clever irony that popped into his thoughts.

"Dick Long, marketing head for Pfizer Drug Company."

"Good afternoon Mr. Switzer. Nice to meet you," Mr. Long said as he threw his hand out to shake.

After Charlie's very lengthy and brilliant presentation, Mr. Long and two of his associates sat in obvious awe. Charles Switzer felt happy and confident. Richard Long agreed to a five-year contract with Charlie, accepting all of his proposals and terms. This would prove to be the most lucrative advertising package ever to be signed. Charlie decided not to stay in New York enjoying the fine restaurants and Broadway shows. Instead, he caught the earliest flight home to begin working immediately.

When the signed contract arrived two days later, Charlie read it twice before signing it. His attorney witnessed and notarized the document before promptly mailing it back overnight. With an executed contract with Pfizer Corporation, Charlie Switzer went home sat down with a tall glass of aged scotch and reread his terms. Although he could not afford the extravagance of expensive liquor, Charlie splurged this time. The Macallan 25 Sherry Cask Highland Single Malt Scotch was smooth, rich, and robust and it was the perfect celebratory drink for Sir Charles. Besides, very soon Charlie would be able to afford to buy this bright amber scotch with a hint of peach, orange, spice, and sherry by the truckload. And he would.

The five-year contract guaranteed Switzer Marketing Company exclusive advertising rights to the Pfizer Pharmaceutical Company's product called (sildenafil citrate) Viagra. After twelve months, if gross sales of Viagra alone did not exceed one hundred million dollars then the contract would be void, and Switzer Marketing would receive no payment. However, if sales did reach one hundred million dollars, Switzer Marketing Co. would receive one-half of one percent of gross sales. After five years the contract would terminate. The five years that followed made Charles Switzer a very rich man. The first year gross sales were over two hundred fifty-nine million dollars. And the fourth and fifth years Viagra sales reached over two billion dollars in annual sales. The Switzer Company received over thirty million dollars in five years of doing business. Of course, after the contract expired, Pfizer immediately broke all ties with Charlie and his company. They had paid royalties for Charlie's expertise and advertising savvy. It was no secret that they could now carry on his campaign without him.

Looking back now, it seemed so simple what Charlie had done to boost sales. He read through his five-year-old strategy many times now. Besides recommending the obvious such as television ads with active couples, often with a tint of gray in their hair, he made a list of words that needed to be changed in all ads. Television, newspapers, billboards, and radio would never use the word impotence. Erectile dysfunction would be the new term. Even though the FDA required drug companies to list all warnings and precautions in all ads, Charlie never used those words. Trying to keep it more positive he referred to the warnings as side effects. But the most ingenious idea from Charlie's imaginative brain came at the end of the list of all the side effects. Charles smiled as he read from his papers.

"Viagra (Sildenafil) is used for the treatment of erectile dysfunction. Common side effects of Viagra include facial flushing, headaches, stomach pain, nasal congestion, nausea, diarrhea, and an inability to differentiate between the colors of green and blue."

Charlie started hysterically laughing out loud thinking who the hell cares if you're color blind with a hard dick. He returned to the list.

"Patients taking nitrates should not take Viagra. Stop using Viagra and call a doctor at once if you have a serious side effect such as:

Sudden vision loss

Ringing in your ears or hearing loss

Chest pain

Nausea, sweating, severe ill feeling

Irregular heartbeat

Swelling in your ankles, hands or feet

Shortness of breath

Vision changes

Feeling light-headed or fainting

Stuffy nose

Memory problems

Back pain."

But it was the last side effect that made Charlie smile because he had invented this side effect. The only side effect that would make every man from eighteen to ninety-nine hungry for the new blue pill.

"In the event of an erection that persists longer than four hours, the patient should seek immediate medical assistance."

"I am a genius," he thought. What male old enough for sex on this earth wouldn't want a hard pecker for four hours?

Charlie's list of side effects was intended to attract customers, not deter them. He felt pretty smug about his creativity until the Food and Drug Administration shot down what he considered the most appealing of all the warnings. Richard Long sent Charlie the FDA message and, in a rare display of humor, added his own comments.

"Mr. Switzer, although very tempting, we cannot permit one of the last items on your warning list as there is no conclusive evidence to support the potential of this reaction."

Charlie was disappointed and imagined the customers he could have had with this home run caution.

"The use of Viagra may cause a penis to permanently extend up to two inches in length and increase by twenty-eight millimeters in girth."

Richard Long added a handwritten note to the FDA letter. "Mr. Switzer, we feel you are stretching it."

Although it did not make sense to him, Charlie was disappointed that both of his concocted side effects were not approved.

"How can having an erection for four hours make more sense than your penis growing a couple inches?" Charlie smiled in spite of himself.

CHAPTER 3

When I arrived in the Keys a few years ago, Limbo was the first friend I made. In fact, we showed up in Key West at exactly the same time. I remember that mid-July four years ago when the weather was hot as hell with no breeze at all. Limbo's job as an undercover customs agent brought him south at the time. I was merely trying to escape a predestined future in the family jewelry business. In my late twenties, I was convinced that being a fishing guide in the Keys would be the perfect life. I was ready to throw all of my education, degrees in business management and marketing along with my gemology degree, out the window in the pursuit of happiness. It did not take long to see the error of my plan. In the Keys, there are thousands of fishing guides. Most of them were more organized and established than I, and all of them were better guides. I knew everything about the jewelry business, gems, gemology, and fashion in the industry but nothing about being a successful guide. My dad had warned me, "You are making a huge mistake son. Stay here in Gulf Breeze and run the family jewelry store."

By the time I realized he was right, I could not admit it, or rather wouldn't admit it.

But thanks to Limbo, his sketchy past, and his questionable work ethics I was able to afford a new start in paradise. In fact, I was able to pay cash for my new home on Cudjoe Key and The Caribbean Jewelry Co. on Duval Street in Key West. Captain Limbo thought that taking a two-million-dollar payoff from his wealthy client who most likely had her husband killed while fishing in the Bahamas was just a well-deserved job benefit.

When I would think about it, which I seldom did, it always sounded more like blackmail to me. Over the years, however, I had come to believe Limbo. For my help on the case, I was entitled to one million dollars which was exactly half of the reward money the widow paid us. After all, reward does indeed sound much better than blackmail payoff.

Since those days, Limbo and I have become as close as brothers. And it was true, we did barely escape death trying to rescue Dawn in Cuba last year. Limbo had saved my life. With plenty of my own regrets, I was eager to hear what was on his mind today.

Limbo chugged the whole bottle of beer, slammed it down on the table, and looked into my eyes.

"I'm not sure she's dead, Powell," he whispered.

"Who?" I replied. Then a chill ran up my spine when I realized what he meant.

"Dawn!" Limbo whispered.

I went numb as my mind raced for an explanation. How can this be? What is he saying? Is it even possible? My thoughts danced in and out of consciousness and my ears went deaf. People around me were still laughing and chatting, the guitarist was holding the microphone to his lips. I heard nothing but an empty echo between my ears. Limbo reached across the table, grabbed my shoulders, and shook me so hard my sunglasses flew across the room. It was as if someone turned up the volume. All of the noises, smells, and sights returned in a split second.

All I could say was, "How can that be possible Limbo? You said you saw her dead body."

"I'm not one hundred percent sure it was her. I saw a young, blonde, dead girl that could have been Dawn, but I knew if we didn't get off that ship we would both die, too. So I told you it was Dawn before I could turn her over and see her face. If you remember, we just barely made it out alive ourselves that night."

My feelings were as confused as his words were. Did I feel relief, hope, or joy? Or did I feel guilt, sorrow, and more pain? Hell, no! What I felt was disbelief, and it highly pissed me off.

"You're full of shit, Limbo! I don't believe a word of this."

CHAPTER 4

A year after his advertising contract ran out with Pfizer Pharmaceutical, Charlie sold Switzer Marketing Company to one of his most loyal employees. Even with all of the millions of dollars in the bank he had made off Viagra, Charlie got top price for his business. Money to Charlie became like bloody waters are to frenzied sharks. Once he got the taste, the hungrier he became. And unfortunately, throughout Charlie's lifetime, this insatiable hunger would never cease.

With his love of the ocean, fishing, and salt air Charlie moved to Fisher Island in Miami that same year. He was now thirty-six years old, a multimillionaire living the perfect dream. But that wasn't good enough for Charlie. He soon became bored.

Charlie opened a high-end funeral home in South Miami selling celebrity funerals. It was an instant success. With Charlie's marketing genius, he hit the lotto once again. His last farewells for the wealthy South Floridians were more like a star-studded TV special. He even had them broadcast on a local television station. The cost of the glamorous television send-off would start at one hundred and fifty thousand dollars. His most impressive funeral, however, was for H. Jonathon Rothschild, III. Although no one really knew who he was when he was alive, his widow was very high maintenance, needing a whole lot of attention while living in her past. She was determined to impress her friends and make a statement. Rothschild was an only child from old money who inherited his billion-dollar fortune from his grandfather, father, and gay uncle who had no children. His wife, Lauren Bergman Rothschild, was a not-so-famous Hollywood movie star back in the fifties. She still lived in that era and enjoyed the lavish lifestyle her husband introduced her to. Charlie picked up on her vulnerability and her need for the spotlight at their first meeting. When he had finished his ingenious interment presentation for H. Jonathan, the Third, the grieving widow's departing words were like poetry to Sir Charles ears.

"And remember Mr. Switzer, money is no object for my late Johnny!" she whispered.

Charlie kept Rothschild's embalmed body on ice for almost two weeks before the funeral arrangements could be finalized. On March twenty-eighth, a Friday night, H. Jonathan Rothschild, III, left this world with a bang. Charlie contacted and hired as many actors and actresses as he could talk into coming. He knew he would not be able to get Tom Hanks, Jack Nicholson, Angelina Jolie, or any other superstars. He started targeting old stars that still had a good name and known face but were now doing reverse mortgage commercials on television. That led him to many greedy, or down-on-their-luck has-been actors and actresses. Charlie advertised the "fun funeral" on national television, local radio stations, Facebook, Twitter, and then followed up with e-vites sent to Miami's most exclusive zip codes. The show started at seven o'clock p.m. with Otis Williams and The Temptations singing "Treat Her Like a Lady." Charlie recommended that song to which the grieving widow enthusiastically agreed. Charlie was still a genius.

The white limousine hearse parked in front of the Setai Hotel in Miami Beach did not dissuade the two thousand close friends and family from saying their goodbye in style. After the Temptations finished their third song, all of the tables were full, the CNN cameras were rolling, and the crab salad was being served to begin the sit-down dinner. The biggest challenge Charlie had was finding a recognizable preacher that was famous, and that would agree to come and say a blessing or two. They had to be somewhat of a celebrity themselves but also be void of shame, credibility, or morality. Charlie reluctantly typed on his computer "preachersforhire.com" and damn, if a site didn't pop up with many possibilities. Their homepage explained that sometimes there is a need for someone to lead a seminar, conduct a service, console an individual, or give an inspirational message. But Charlie had no luck here. Each rent-a-preacher he called was appalled at the morbid idea of speaking at a stranger's televised funeral service as if he were a close friend. But one night Charlie was sipping his third martini while watching the national news, and like divine intervention, there he was. A well-recognized reverend and the master of racial profiteering was visiting the site of a terrible tragedy trying to console "his people." But while there, on national television, he asked the grieving families to donate money to his church. He had traveled a long distance to console his flock, and now it was time for them to show their gratitude. In one short phone call, Charlie had hired his devout yet unscrupulous man of the cloth.

Tonight the crowd was joyous. The stage was set for entertainment and sharing fond memories, most of which would be made up. Six steps led up to the stage. To the left was a lighted pulpit and to the right, a twenty-piece band. The center of the stage was open for the show, with many movie cameras rolling back and forth catching the stars' most photogenic sides. At the base of the stairs in an open casket lay H. Jonathan Rothschild, III. There was a constant revolving light show that lit up the sensationalized crypt like a Broadway show. Charlie couldn't help but think that the green, red, and blue lighting that flickered and bounced across Johnny's face was like the fucking Aurora Borealis.

Rothschild was dressed in a black and white tuxedo with a white bow tie, black cummerbund, blue sapphire studs and diamond and sapphire cuff links all set in platinum. Because of too much time sitting dead in the funeral home waiting for tonight, he required heavy layers of makeup on his face and lips. The contrasting gray skin tones with very red lips made him look like Jack Nicholson's rendition of the Joker in Batman. As each person came up to the coffin to pay their respects, every reaction was the same—obscene laughter!

As the salads were set on the tables, the preacher took the pulpit and began to bless the food and say a few words about his dear friend Jonathon. Charlie had paid him well for his message, along with generous travel expenses from D.C. and advised him not to "pass the basket" to this crowd.

"I am proud to be here to say goodbye to my longtime dear friend Jonathon Rothfield."

Everyone in the room was so surprised to see Reverend Al Jackson on stage, they didn't notice he got the dead man's name wrong. The evening flowed nicely with the gracious, actress-like widow walking proudly from table to table thanking each and every one for being there to support her in her time of sorrow. The sounds from the dance routines from almost recognizable groups often drowned out her conversations. But it was during the main entrees and dessert that became the widow's favorite part of the evening. All of her fellow actors and actresses would say a few words. Charlie's list was an impressive one. He only hoped they got his name right while the television cameras were on. Although Al Jackson was a hard act to follow, Nick Nolte, Charro, Jan-Michael Vincent, Lee Majors, Gary Busey, Pat Boone, Shirley Jones, Loni Anderson, and Burt Reynolds were magnificent with their heartfelt eulogies. After dinner, they rolled the casket to the center of the dance floor. Jonathon the Joker's eyes seemed to follow the drunk couples as they slid across the waxed terrazzo floor.

At two in the morning, after everyone had left, the widow went to the side of her deceased husband to say her last farewell and thank him for tonight's party. Charlie gave her a moment alone with Jonathon before closing the casket and returning him to the funeral home for tomorrow's burial. The widow began to weep loudly and then scream. Charlie thought it very unusual since she had shown no emotions since his death. He ran to her side. She was holding his hand sobbing.

"What's wrong Mrs. Rothschild?" Charlie asked.

She held up Jonathon's right hand to show Charlie his thumb was missing. Charlie's only concern was why the hell she was grabbing his hands and arms. He quickly explained that the embalming fluid entrance is at your thumb. She was so tired, drunk, and exhausted that she not only bought it, she was relieved.

Lauren Rothschild had the time of her life tonight. Writing the check for just under two million dollars was not a problem for the billionaire widow. After all the expenses for flowers, limo, hotel conference room, music, food, the famous preacher, and all of Lauren's actor friends were paid, Charlie cleared eight hundred thousand dollars. He was the master. Charlie's new found life of rubbing elbows with the rich and famous seemed to fit his style. He soon realized that the rich, the celebrities, and the fashionistas were easy targets for a guilt trip. And Lauren Rothschild was no different. She was happy to pay dearly for her deceased Jonathon and even more so for her own absolution! Greed had treated Charlie well, at least for now.

CHAPTER 5

Because of a very busy day ahead, I was up early this morning. I ground some fresh dark roast coffee beans from Baby's Coffee and brewed up a very strong pot. As I was pouring my first cup, I heard a car in my driveway and then the sound of my daily paper hitting the front door. Still dark with a full hour before the sunrise, I retrieved the *Key West Times* and retreated upstairs to my back deck. The air was a fragrant mixture of salt and monkey shit. Due south on the ocean side only two miles from where I sit is Key Lois. Formerly known as Cayavama Key, Loggerhead Key, and later Key Lois, it now is referred to as Monkey Island. The entire Key was the site of a commercially operated breeding colony of rhesus monkeys. The monkeys were used as unwilling test subjects and roamed freely among the mangroves of Key Lois. It is said that many boaters, fisherman, and curious tourists were attacked by the angry primates over the years. The free roaming monkeys also destroyed half of the island, stripping it bare of any vegetation. Finally, in 1999, the whole operation was determined to be inhumane and was ordered to close down. And although the leaves and vegetation have returned to the mangroves, whenever a strong southeast wind blows, the sour stench of monkey shit hovers over Cudjoe Key. Today was one of those days.

I glanced through the paper quickly thinking it was another typical news day in Key West. A commercial lobster fisherman had shot his boss with a spear gun on Stock Island. Quite a few people were fined for harvesting illegal lobster that were too short. A woman went missing from a cruise ship when it docked at Mallory Square. And then there was the normal night of fights, public intoxication, indecent exposure, and debauchery that has made Duval Street one of the most popular streets in America. But the only new and interesting headline read, "Miami Billionaire's Bank Account Robbed Two Days After His Funeral!" The thing that was so intriguing was that the sophisticated thief was able to pass a high-tech computerized fingerprint scanner to access the man's five-million-dollar-petty cash account that they cleaned out.

The article caught my eye and concerned me because the deceased billionaire banked at South Beach Bank and Trust in Miami. And I did all of my banking here in Key West at the satellite location. What was worse was that I had just updated my business and personal accounts to all fingerprint scanned access.

I met with the bank officers and asked many questions before switching over the accounts. They assured me it was the most secure and safe choice. They told me instead of a password, you only need your distinctive print to gain access. I was a little hesitant, so I researched it thoroughly. No two fingerprints are alike, even in identical twins. The scanning process starts when you place your finger on a glass plate. The fingerprint scanner then can determine whether the pattern of ridges and valleys in the image matches the pattern in your pre-scanned images. It is absolutely very high-end technology and totally foolproof. So I wondered, how did someone bypass the system and steal five million dollars from Miami billionaire H. Jonathon Rothschild, III, after he was six feet under? I began to question this whole fingerprint technology because there had to be a simple explanation. My mind was a vacuum filled with questions, speculations, and conjecture. Could scanners distinguish between a picture of a finger and the finger itself? Could a mold be made of a finger while the person was asleep? Or even worse, could a criminal cut off somebody's finger to get past a scanner security system? Stop! I told myself. The old geezer probably had some young girlfriend on the side that had access somehow.

Although this was all very intriguing, it was beginning to get light outside, and I was running late. I would need to hurry if I was going to make it to work in time to my meet my customer.

CHAPTER 6

Charlie's hard work and creative marketing genius along with Lady Luck allowed him a lifestyle most people only dreamed of. With plenty of money in the bank, a huge home on Fisher Island in Miami and another waterfront home in Key West, most people would be happy and content. Not Charlie!

His celebrity funeral home was so successful he decided to open a branch in Key West. It only made sense that since he had homes in both cities and was on a bank board that operated in both Miami and Key West, he should spend more time in the southernmost city of the U.S. Besides, he loved to shark fish, and there is no place better on earth to hunt bull sharks than off Key West. Charlie had recently come into a little more cash, so he decided to use it wisely. He bought a vacant building on Duval Street to be headquarters for his funeral home. He donated one million dollars to the Tennessee Williams Fine Arts Center at Florida Keys Community College on Stock Island. He gave another million dollars to Key West Maritime Historical Society and to the Theatre of the Sea Marine Life Park in Islamorada. He then bought himself a forty-five-foot SeaVee "Fish Around" boat with three Yamaha 350's. And lastly, he purchased a lady's eight-carat diamond ring for an ex-girlfriend he was trying to entice back. That ate up all of the five million dollars he recently came into.

As smart as Charlie was, he miscalculated the need for another funeral home in Key West. It took less than a week of research to realize that most people who died in Key West were from somewhere else and their bodies were returned home for funerals. Also, there is no land left in Key West for burials. Once again Charlie's marketing imagination kicked into high gear.

The grand opening was set for the end of April in a new location on Duval Street for the Southernmost Sea Burial & Cremation Company.

Charlie's six-page color brochure explaining the available services looked like a handout you would get in Key West on the corner of Duval and Greene Street. It was beautifully done. Southernmost Sea Burial & Cremation Company also had a state-of-the-art website. Charlie was convinced that people all over the United States who had ever visited the Keys would surely want their loved one scattered off the southernmost point of America. Charlie had many burial packages to fit the need of any deceased.

His basic sea burial started at two hundred dollars which was a no thrills, unattended scattering of the cremated remains. He called it the Sea Gull Package. All the customer had to do was ship or bring by their loved one's ashes in the original box from the crematory along with a copy of the release form. They would also need a copy of the death certificate and a cashier's check made out to Southernmost Sea Burial, LLC for two hundred dollars. Any photographs, GPS coordinates, or engraved urns were all extra charges. In the brochure and on the website under the heading Sea Gull Package, it stated, "honorable and affordable way to commemorate the life of a loved one." Below that was a picture of a breathtaking sunset over the ocean with a couple of hibiscus flowers floating on the surface and a sky filled with seagulls. Truly, this picture was worth a thousand words.

"If people only knew the reality," Charlie thought to himself.

Charlie did only cremation burials at sea. Full body burials in the ocean were a hassle. There were just too many obstacles, like having metal caskets, the Coast Guard approval forms, body inspections and identification and fuel expenses to take the body far enough out to be in six hundred feet of water. But burials at sea for cremated remains were quite easy. They could be scattered at any depth as long as it was three miles from land. As long as the Environmental Protection Agency was notified in writing thirty days prior, there would never be problems.

For the entry-level sea burial, Charlie had cleverly rigged his Jet

Ski to hold up to ten boxes of loved ones' remains. Owning a funeral home with a crematorium certainly helped with logistics. To save time and fuel Charlie would wait until he had at least what he called a six-pack, before heading out. He would place the boxes on a shelf he built under the seat in a waterproof hatch. About an hour before sunset Charlie would launch the Jet Ski at Garrison Bight Marina, go out of the channel and head south past Mallory Square. He loved to watch all of the tourists that showed up nightly for the sunset and traditional party. Bikini-clad babes always yelled and waved at Charlie when he slowly passed too close to the docks. But then again, he was hard to miss. The colorful WaveRunner was painted white, with light blue seagulls on the sides accompanied by decals a little darker blue that read: Au Revoir, Sayonara, Adios, Ciao, Farewell and—Charlie's favorite—Nashle. A beautiful girl he dated from the Czech Republic screamed that at him one night after an ugly argument. Never hearing from her again Charlie assumed it meant goodbye.

After cruising by Mallory Square, Charlie would head due south the three miles necessary to scatter the remains. He would kill the engine and float around as he prepared the burial site. If photographs were included, he would toss out three plastic hibiscus flowers, all shades of red and pink. Next, he would throw out a chum bag to attract the seagulls, thus the source for the name of this particular sea burial package. Charlie actually took the photos of the sunset, floating plastic, and hovering seagulls before he dumped the loved ones overboard. If not, the pictures would have shown a flock of frenzied, ravenous birds eating the powdered remains of poor ole Aunt Bessie from Minneapolis.

The round trip to the sea buoy cost about three dollars in fuel and a couple dollars for chum. A full load of deceased remains would bring two thousand dollars for an hour's work. Good pay for some, but not for Charlie. He didn't do it for the money. Besides, he already had more money than he could ever spend. Charlie could not control his obsessive desire to possess wealth, objects, or anything with value. Greed thrived in his bloodstream.

Other more profitable choices in the Southernmost Sea Burial & Cremation Company brochure included an assortment of packages where the loved ones could participate. For these more extravagant customers, Charlie would dress up in a nice blue dress shirt with Khaki pants and a captain's hat he bought on Duval Street. Using his new SeaVee boat, not only was it impressive but he could take up to twenty mourners with him. The dolphin watch was one of the most popular choices. Families could observe dolphins frolicking in the boat's wake on the way out. And for only one hundred dollars more Charlie would set them up with rods and reels to troll for dinner. This was a four-hour trip, and the total package cost four hundred fifty dollars per person. If they had not caught any fish before scattering the ashes, Charlie would take them by a wreck on the way in where barracuda always would bite. But Charlie's favorite burial package was the Environmental Trip. He had bird lists printed up where the family could check off all of the seabirds they saw. He rented them binoculars and on a good day would see thirty to forty different species of birds. On almost all of the trips, the clients bought the t-shirts. He had two choices of colorful T's. One had a cross floating on the ocean with dolphins jumping over it and seagulls gliding through the sky as the sun set. The other was exactly the same, but no cross, for all non-Christian religions. Over the beautiful art was "S.S.B & C.", and underneath simply read "Charon's Retired." Luckily, no one so far had read Dante's *Inferno*, and if asked, Charlie would say Charon was his mother. Charlie also made some extra cash with retail items. He sold everything from sunscreen, hats, sunglasses, and beautiful engraved urns to flowers and wreaths that were readily decomposable in the marine environment.

CHAPTER 7

Luckily the traffic was light into Key West this morning. After Limbo's recent revelations, I was having a hard time concentrating on business. Even though I was running behind schedule, I decided to stop at mile marker fifteen and grab a café con leche at Baby's Coffee. It was early enough that I did not have to wait in line for Olga to steep the large bold Cuban brew.

By the time I reached Caribbean Jewelers on Duval Street, I was quite wired from the high dose of caffeine. However, I was not certain if my nervous jitters were caused by the coffee or the important new customer I was to meet. The unlikely possibility of Dawn still being alive kept nagging at me as well.

Devin Drake, my manager for the store, has been with me since the very beginning when I acquired Caribbean Jewelers three years ago. Devin was born on Ramrod Key and spent her entire thirty-six years in the Keys except for the four years in Gainesville while attending college. Because of her older brother Gilbert, she always loved to fish. He was a famous Keys tarpon guide that reached celebrity status in his earlier years while escorting the more elite fly fisherman in their quest to land a tarpon on fly.

Their father had opened a well-known bonefish lodge in the Bahamas during the fifties. The entire family, including Devin, had fished with many of the greatest sportsmen of our times. The impressive list included artists, musicians, authors, actors, royalty, and even presidents. So it was no mystery as to why Devin never left the Keys. It was in her blood.

I met Devin at No Name Pub on Big Pine Key late one evening soon after I acquired Caribbean Jewelers. The restaurant was so crowded that night Dawn and I were seated at her table. When asked by the waitress if she minded sharing her table Devin snapped, "Fuck no, I don't mind! The more fucking people, the better!" She introduced us to her girlfriend and very soon I realized she could throw the F-bomb between syllables with a charmed ease that Dawn and I found pretty amusing.

"Candace is my girlfriend. We are gay, you know, lesbian. If that fucking bothers you, we understand. If not, let's get another fucking pitcher of Yuengling," Devin announced to puzzled expressions. The four of us left when they closed the bar down after way too many pitchers of beer to recall.

Devin is about five-foot-two with a burned hide that has baked in the tropical sun her entire life. She weighs all of ninety pounds when she is soaking wet and full of Yuenglings. She is a true Key Western, a Conch, as people native to the Keys are called. Applying for the job she assured me she could bite her sailor's tongue from eight to five while in the jewelry store. That was almost three years ago. Devin is a great manager, gemologist, and an out-of-the-closet lesbian that knows how to treat customers. We have been through a lot in those three short years. I would trust my life and my store with her.

When Devin phoned yesterday to inform me about my appointment with a new customer, she was a bit vague. All she knew was that a man named Charlie had asked to meet with me about purchasing a large diamond engagement ring. Growing up in my dad's jewelry store I worked hard and studied hard to learn everything I could about the business. Armed with that experience along with my education in gemology, management, and marketing I was ready to meet with Charlie.

I arrived at the store a customary fifteen minutes early. When I walked in, the sales room was very crowded and busy. Devin forced a side-eyed glance my way rolling her eyes towards a man in the diamond room. She smiled and nodded letting me know Charlie had arrived early as well.

I was quite impressed with Charlie Switzer. He was well-dressed, well-groomed, articulate, and had certainly done his homework on diamonds. He was very professional and genuinely likable. For the first hour, we spoke about diamonds and only diamonds. I felt like I was being graded for my final exam in gemology class. After I explained clarity, cut, and color qualities along with showing him different sizes and shapes Charlie decided on a beautiful ring, but not until he examined it under the microscope with a jeweler's attention to detail while asking a hundred questions. Once Charlie finally accepted my explanations and agreed with my clarifications, he decided on a stone. The 8.02 carat emerald-cut diamond that measured 14.15 by 10.46 by 6.36 mm and had a GIA Certificate was an exceptional choice. The color was G (near colorless) with an internally flawless clarity. The proportions of the cut made it more magnificent. For the second hour, while our jewelers were setting and sizing the ring in platinum with two one-and-a-half-carat trapezoid diamonds on each side, Charlie and I got to know each other better. I gave him a quick background on myself, my credentials, and how I came to own Caribbean Jewelers. I left out plenty of details.

Although sixteen years separate Charlie Switzer and me, we both grew up only a few miles from each other in the Florida Panhandle. A three-mile bridge across Pensacola Bay divides Pensacola from Gulf Breeze. Charlie stayed in Pensacola's Escambia County while I moved to Gulf Breeze's Santa Rosa County at age ten. It is quite interesting that now, twenty years later, the two of us meet in Key West a city on the opposite end of the state from where we hail.

I was correct with my first impression of Charlie. He was indeed an interesting man. He told me how he made his money advertising Viagra in the early stages of product development, his successful funeral business in Miami and now Key West along with his involvement as a board member at the South Beach Bank & Trust of Miami. He also was very happy and animated telling me the story of his most famous funeral, that of one H. Jonathon Rothschild, III. I recognized the name from the article in the *Key West Times* I had just read. I thought it quite odd and a coincidence that the man who marketed a two-million-dollar funeral, performing the ceremony himself, was also on the board of the bank where someone stole five million dollars from the deceased the next day. I did not want to pursue the conversation today. The ring was completed, set, sized, and pol-ished. And what a spectacular engagement ring it was. Charlie Switzer had no problem writing the check for eight hundred ninety-nine thousand, six hundred and fifty dollars. And I certainly had no issue with accepting it.

I made one short stop on the ride back home to Cudjoe Key. I had a celebratory beer at the New Joint Lounge above the Square Grou-per restaurant. I happily toasted my newest wealthy customer and friend Charlie Switzer. I could have easily nestled into my bar stool and ordered quite a few more brews. The bar was busy with plenty of noise, laughter, live music, chatter and the excited screams of a young couple as they slid a puck in each other's direction on a shuffle bowling machine. I decided not to stay this night. A quiet deck, a sunset, and a bottle of red were all calling me home.

CHAPTER 8

When the phone rang, Powell Taylor was sitting on his deck overlooking Cudjoe Bay. Ignoring the annoying rings of the telephone, he sat in an old church pew that found its way to his canal after Hurricane Wilma in '05. Bleached by the sun and pitted from its ocean journey, the pew was unique but hardly comfortable. The wooden treasure was a gift from the previous homeowner. On many nights, fond memories returned of the times when he and Dawn sat there with a glass of port in hand. He could recall every single setting of the sun that faded into a long sleep before disappearing off towards Bone Island.

Tonight, as Powell struggled with sad memories of Dawn's disappearance, a half moon was rising in the wake of a dramatic sunset. The fiery orange and red neon layering was still visible in the western sky over Key West. The subdued white light of the partial moon caught his eye from the east. A blue heron stood four feet tall just a couple yards from Powell's bare feet. A noisy fish crow squawked with anger as it perched above the roof over his skiff. There was just enough light from the horizon and the piece of moon to see a pair of dolphin chasing a school of mullet towards shallow water. The silver scales of the airborne fish caught the light of the moon as they fled for safety. When they swam out of sight, Powell closed his eyes and listened to the tumultuous roar of the turbulent waters. His mind pictured the dolphins feeding with acrobatic precision. He heard their tails slap the bay's surface, flipping a mullet out of the water before turning to grab the stunned prey with their mouth. It was a dinner bell he had heard many times over the years. And then there was dead silence. As the tide fell, the dolphins continued their journey to the mouth of the bay. The lucky surviving mullet found safety around the pilings of the many boat docks that littered the shore.

It was less than a year ago when things were best between Powell and Dawn that the couple sat here together until the early morning hours. Powell told her stories of how life was growing up back home on the opposite end of Florida. The city of Gulf Breeze is surrounded by saltwater on three sides. It was on Pensacola Bay where Powell was raised fishing, crabbing, throwing a cast net, and exploring the coast in his sixteen-foot-fiberglass skiff with a ten-horse Johnson outboard. That may have been his favorite form of transportation still to date. Powell caught himself smiling with the recollection of those early years, the years he often referred to as his ten-horse education. Powell felt he learned more from the many hours he spent in that skiff than all of the twelve years of Catholic education and the four years at Florida State University combined.

At the young age of ten his dad, Charles Sr., had introduced Powell to the greatest educational environment on earth. His father's tutelage was more by accident than a well-thought-out plan. But the first time the two of them took the skiff out, Powell knew his dad was brilliant. Charles Sr. spent most of his time working in the family jewelry store, so Powell never missed a chance to run the skiff, usually alone.

Although many people have tried to take the credit, it was Mark Twain who first penned the phrase, "I never let schooling interfere with my education." The literary genius only made it through elementary school, but because of his self-education he still became known as the "Father of America Literature."

Every day Powell could not wait to jump off the school bus and run down the old wooden cypress dock to his boat. He hopped aboard the skiff, tied to an old creosote piling, and pumped the rubber ball on the gas tank while pulling on the choke. Usually, it only took one tug on the pull cord to make the engine purr like a kitten. Powell would twist and hold the throttle arm so hard on the highest speed that often his hand would cramp up. His classroom consisted of a fifteen-mile radius of Pensacola Bay, the Gulf of Mexico, and the Intercostal Waterway. His school desk was sixteen feet long, painted white with a wide blue stripe. The bow light was busted, the transom had begun to rot, but time stood still whenever he sat at its stern steering his childhood chariot.

The boat was heavy and slow but that never bothered Powell. The thirty-minute trek to run three miles to the Gulf of Mexico taught him much. Over the years while in the sun on his skiff, he studied everything the marine environment had to offer. Every day was an adventure, an experience. It was not long before Powell knew more about tidal flow, wind shifts and patterns, gravitational pull of the moon and sun, and the difference between diurnal and semi-diurnal tides than his sixth-grade teacher ever knew. One the fondest memories of his elementary years was when Ms. Cibula asked him to explain local shore birds. Powell was always fascinated by birds, even from a very early age. He would sit for hours and watch them come and go to his mother's feeders in the back yard. For Christmas, in the first grade, he asked Santa Claus for a pair of binoculars and a book on birds. So he was very excited to tell his classmates and his favorite teacher, Ms. Cibula, all about the bird life he loved on Pensacola Bay. His youthful eleven-year-old passion was obvious as well as contagious. His classmates sat very still as he told stories of diving gulls and terns picking minnows off the surface near the big bluffs. He told them how an osprey grabbed a mullet from a school near Fort Pickens and all about the shorebird behavior near the jetties in the Gulf. They also loved hearing about the clumsy attack of the brown pelican as he smashed into the water head first after his prey. But their favorite story was also Powell's favorite. Once while he was fishing the pilings around the Bay Bridge for sheepshead, he kept seeing a bird fly up high and drop something into the Holiday Inn parking lot. He pulled over closer, threw out his anchor, and watched the unusual and peculiar ceremony. A very large light-gray and white gull with dull pink legs that he would later discover was a herring gull, would grab an oyster from the shoreline, fly straight up high over the asphalt parking lot and suddenly drop the shell. The bird would follow it down, stand beside it, and eat the bruised mollusk from the cracked shell.

"Wow!" one of the kids yelled. "Who taught it that?" she asked.

Powell stood speechless. He did not know the answer, but neither did Ms. Cibula. Powell spent so much time in his boat by summer's end his skin was stained and burnt cinnamon. And without pain, the sea's salt would stick to his blistered back like pelican shit on a buoy. When Powell started high school, he had his doctorate in ten-horse education. He studied crustaceans and mollusks, knew why mullet jump, and even knew that sixty-five percent of mullet fall on their left side when re-entering the water. Powell could tell when the wind direction was about to change, or the tide would neap and could predict a squall, hurricane, or extreme tide better than Jim Cantore. By studying daily on the bay, he became a phenomenal fisherman, first with a cast net, then with a spinning rod and finally he mastered the fly rod. On each and every day's adventures, Powell always managed to return to the dock only minutes before the sun would set over Pensacola Bay. And that is why even now, it is still his favorite time of the day.

When his cell phone rang again, Powell jumped up as if suddenly awakened from a deep sleep. It was late, the sun had long been set. Powell grabbed the phone and put it to his ear. Before he could answer, he heard a voice call out, "Powell! Powell! Is that you?"

His head started to pound, he could feel the blood leave his face. "Dawn! Is that you?"

And then a familiar voice screamed out, "Dawn? What the fuck are you talking about? It's Devin. What's up, Powell?"

"Nothing, let's talk later," he said while hanging up the phone. A few minutes later he wondered why Devin was calling, but not enough to call her back.

By now he had put a good dent in a bottle of a fine cabernet and decided to smoke a Cohiba that he brought back from one of his trips to Havana. The mix of red wine and fine Cuban tobacco along with the evening salt air is a magical combination that, like Powell, most watermen appreciate. Powell positioned himself as comfortably as possible in the old church pew and thought about Dawn. He never imagined this. And he now found himself so unprepared. Just when Powell started to accept the fact that Dawn was gone forever and his guilt had finally begun to subside, every memory of the time he and Dawn spent together was back.

Not knowing whether she was alive or dead may have been worse than his accepting her death. Ever since Limbo suggested that Dawn may still be alive, Powell found himself looking and searching crowds in the hopes of catching a glimpse of her. The other day while he walked up Duval Street after work, he stopped in Sloppy Joe's for a beer. The entire time he scanned the crowded bar as if by some strange miracle Dawn would appear. Someone called out his name. He turned quickly expecting to see his past love dressed in her usual bikini, cover-up and sandals holding up a salted margarita while dancing to the music coming from the packed stage of local musicians. It was not Dawn at all but one of his salesgirls from the jewelry store. Powell hoped she had not noticed the sudden change in his facial expression going from joyous expectation to sheer disappointment.

CHAPTER 9

I was up early with a throbbing headache behind my eyes. Too much vino and inhaling the strong Cohiba last night were to blame. As I drove into the parking lot of Five Brothers Grocery on Ramrod Key, my phone rang. I saw it was Devin calling from the jewelry store. Since I ran out of coffee at home and had not yet had my morning cup, I decided I would wait and call her after I did.

I ordered a café con leche and a Cuban breakfast sandwich. Both were great as always. I sat outside in their parking lot under a coconut palm and enjoyed the egg, bacon, and cheese pressed between Cuban bread while soaking up the morning light. My phone began to ring again. This time I answered her. "Yes Devin, what is so important this early?"

"Well, after last night when you thought I was Dawn calling from the grave I was a little concerned. What the fuck, Powell?" she snapped.

"Don't cuss at work Devin and don't worry about last night. I'll explain later," I answered.

"Okay! Okay!" she said. "Also, Charlie Switzer, the guy that bought the big fucking diamond yesterday—"

"What?" I scolded.

"I mean that gentleman that bought that beautiful and rather large ring yesterday. Better?"

"Yes, just watch your mouth at work, please," I replied.

"He invited you and me to dinner tonight at seven thirty at Santiago's Bodega."

"What does he want?" I asked.

"He was in the store yesterday after you left and we had an incident with a customer. But before you get excited, it was no big deal. Some big fat ass woman— Oh wait, I mean a very large, portly lady slipped and fell. She's okay, but what drama. I'll fill you in later," Devin said.

"Can't wait! Tell him okay, and I'll meet you at the restaurant about seven so we'll be prepared before Charlie arrives," I said.

I hung up and drove back home. When I turned the corner onto Buccaneer Lane, I could see Woodrow's stained driver's side in my driveway. Knowing Limbo had come by for a visit made me happy. Limbo has been a good friend to me for all of my years here in the Keys, and he had helped me more than once. He has risked his life for me and had most definitely saved my life last year in Havana. I owe Limbo more than I could ever repay.

I still did not know what was up with him, or if he really knew if Dawn was alive or dead, but it was good to see my friend again.

Although Limbo has a key to my house, I could not find him inside. I looked upstairs and out on the back deck. I finally spotted him swimming in the canal behind the boathouse that held my Maverick skiff.

"Hey, Limbo!" I yelled from the deck. "What's up?"

"Not much, just had to soak for a little bit. Needed some saltwater on my skin. It's been awhile," he replied.

Limbo's past was still a mystery to me. In all of his fifty years, I know he had some secret military experiences that he never speaks of. I also know when we first met years ago on our way to the Keys, he worked undercover with U.S. Customs. And somewhere in the years between, Limbo got his doctorate in marine biology. Anyone who would see him now would have no idea that this old six-foot-two-inch, lanky, hippie-like, fishing, beach bum would have such an impressive résumé and interesting background. The sun has done a number on him over the years. His hair is bleached white, his hide is a sunburned coffee color, and his nose, ears, and back are scarred from numerous skin cancers he had removed. And yet he still worships the sun and saturates himself in the salty waters daily. His fit but wrinkled body touched by the sun's rays matches his age.

I grabbed a six-pack of Fat Tire from the cooler and lowered my skiff into the water. The sound from the boat lift drowned out what Limbo was saying. When the boat came to rest I heard Limbo repeat, "We going fishing, Powell?"

"No, thought we'd just take a ride over to Little Palm Island, drink a couple of beers and catch up," I said.

"Great plan, Powell. Let's go!"

I idled out of the canal into Cudjoe Bay, brought the skiff up on plane and followed the channel south. Once in the ocean, I headed southeast around Monkey Island towards Little Palm. The wind was more than slight out of the south, so we luckily were spared the smell of monkey shit. When we pulled up to the dock on Little Palm, the ferry that brings the lucky tourists to and from the island was just departing for the mainland. The attractive deckhand dressed in white shorts, a pink Polo shirt and deck shoes helped us tie up the skiff. She then escorted us to the beachside bar. Limbo and I sat at a table in the sand on the water's edge while the tiny Key deer curiously walked up to us hoping for a tasty handout. The hours passed quickly and without notice as we engrossed ourselves in conversation that was long overdue.

By the time we left the island and returned back home to Cudjoe Key, we had discussed many topics. I told him of my concerns with the fat lady who fell in my store. He convinced me to call my insurance company and prepare them just in case. I agreed. We talked about Charlie Switzer and both of our concerns about him. Although neither of us knew why, we did not feel totally comfortable around Charlie. And lastly, we discussed Dawn, her disappearance last year, our attempt to save her and the possibility that she may have escaped alive. It was too much to comprehend after a few beers and a boat ride. It was after five when I got the skiff put up, so I had to hurry if I was going to meet Charlie and Devin in Key West by seven.

CHAPTER 10

I decided to bring Limbo with me tonight. There were no parking spaces anywhere near Santiago's Bodega so I parked eight blocks away in Bahama Village and we walked to the restaurant. The place was packed. I found Devin at a back table with a glass of cheap rosé wine.

"I'm not working. So how was your fucking day?" she said with a big laugh.

"Great, so far," I replied, "Is that about to change?"

"Well, maybe. Good to see you again, Limbo," she said.

"Same here, Devin!" Limbo answered.

Limbo and I each ordered a beer while Devin caught me up on the incident with the lady that fell and hit her head on a jewelry case while shopping yesterday.

"That fat bitch is a fake!" Devin excitedly yelled out. "I guarantee you she'll be back."

"Calm down," I said.

Devin explained that the lady was very elderly, overweight, very loud, and extremely obnoxious.

"Where's your girlfriend Candy?" I asked.

"Her name is Candace, Candace Kane. Nobody fucking calls her Candy for the obvious reason," she snapped. "And she is not here because I did not invite her. I didn't feel like she should know all of your business," she added to my delight.

I let her know how much I appreciated her concerns and confidentiality before asking her, "What does Charlie Switzer want to talk about tonight?"

"Do I look like a fucking mind reader?" she quipped.

As many times as Devin drops the F-bomb, I still am caught off-guard every time, but it always makes me laugh aloud, no matter how hard I try not to. Sometimes I am sure she uses the foul language just to get a reaction from me. We ordered two more beers and another glass of rosé before Charlie Switzer showed up at precisely seven thirty.

Charlie's friendly, inviting demeanor put everyone at ease the second he arrived.

"Good to see you again, Powell," he said as he threw out his hand to squeeze. "And you look as beautiful as ever, Devin," he continued.

I held my breath waiting for her colorful reply that I feared would be something like, "Go fuck yourself in the eye and quit blowing smoke up my gay ass, Charlie." But luckily Devin was truly in her working mode when she replied, "Thank you, so nice to see you again, Mr. Switzer."

Relieved, I exhaled a little too loudly when I forced the trapped air from my lungs. I introduced Charlie and Limbo to one another. They shook hands and exchanged a few words before Charlie sat down to join us. Within seconds our waitress showed up with a huge smile.

"Mr. Switzer, I didn't know you were joining us tonight. I'm so glad to see you again. The usual to drink?"

He grinned and nodded while he answered, "Yes Lisa, that would be great. I appreciate it."

It was if Lisa had just received general absolution for life from the Most Holy Pope himself. She took off towards the bar skipping and singing like a ten-year-old.

Charlie sure had a way with people. That was undeniable. But there was something I just did not trust about him, although I could not put my finger on it. I didn't know why I felt that way, as he certainly had never given me any reason. Still, he reminded me of a smooth con artist, a charlatan, or maybe even a television evangelist.

Lisa brought Charlie's mojito in a tall glass, light on the ice, heavy on the rum and sugar made with the Cuban mint hierbabuena, not the usual spearmint. He tasted it, made a sigh of joy and announced, "Perfect," as he slapped her butt. Lisa ran off towards the kitchen, giggling out of control. When she quickly returned, we ordered a variety of tapas for the table to share along with a few more rounds of drinks.

"Her name is Hilda Tucker," Charlie exclaimed while sipping his fifth Mojito.

"I thought you said her name was Lisa," I answered.

"Not this cute little waitress, Powell, the big fat woman that fell in your store yesterday." The fraud, Hilda Tucker.

I didn't respond immediately. I just stared at him, a little unnerved by his intrusiveness. My first thought was to tell him to mind his own business, stay out of it, and that I would handle it, but curiosity got the best of me. How and why would Charlie be involved with this woman? Why would he care at all? I was about to ask exactly that when I glanced over at Devin. She looked like she had been caught with her hand in the jewelry jar. Her exaggerated expression of guilt lit up her red face like an August sunburn. I suddenly knew where Charlie got his information. We had her name, address, and phone number in our computer's customer list, all confidential of course. I would save that conversation with Devin for a later, more private, time. I was glad Lisa showed up with our order, breaking the awkward silence at the table. Limbo had not said a word since Charlie sat down with us, and Devin was staring off into midair, numb to our presence.

"Who ordered the seared tuna?" Lisa interrupted. "How about the scallops and goat cheese? And the cracked conch?" she added.

During the last hour of dining, we managed to make small talk, finish our dinner, and schedule a fishing trip. I felt as if Charlie had much more information he wanted to share with us tonight on Hilda Tucker. However, I was not interested in hearing it now, so I kept changing the subject each time he brought it up. I did want to know more about her but would rather get the complete story when there was less of an audience.

Finally, after realizing I did not want to discuss the fat lady, Charlie dropped it then invited us to fish the weekend on his new SeaVee. Limbo and I agreed. The amount of alcohol we had consumed had more to do with accepting than actually wanting to fish. I was sure I would regret the decision before Sunday.

We said our goodbyes and thanked Charlie for dinner. I told Devin I looked forward to talking with her soon. She grunted, turned, and stumbled to the sidewalk. Limbo drove me home.

I knew that falling asleep anytime soon tonight was out of the question. If I tried, my mind would spin in many directions. Besides thoughts of Dawn, lawsuits, fat women, Limbo, and my jewelry store, I now could add Charlie Switzer's obsession with Hilda Tucker to the list of reasons for my insomnia. But as I often do on those evenings where I find myself unable to doze off, I remedy my recurrent malady with a glass of port and a good read. For this reason, I keep a supply of good books handy. I enjoy most fiction novels, murder mysteries, and some non-fiction books. So, I always have plenty of each nearby. I fear that being without good reading material, I may stay up all night staring at the ceiling with my brain working overtime focusing on negative thoughts. Tonight I picked the perfect book to calm my head. It would not be the first time I read *On The Water*. The author, a Frenchman, lives happily on his farm in North Florida surrounded by a twenty-seven-acre pond, secluded woods, and his wild creatures. Although his enchanting memoirs are compelling stories centered around different bodies of water and his favorite hunting grounds, they are of great interest to me. His beautifully written lyrical prose clears and calms my mind. I fell into a deep sleep around chapter six, with my last meditation-like thoughts not about Hilda the Hun or Charlie Switzer.

CHAPTER 11

My Darling Powell,

Where do I start? I guess the first and most important thing is to let you know how much I love you and how sorry I am for everything that has happened. I have had plenty of time in the past seven months to reflect on my life, my mistakes, and most importantly, my love for you. This writing comes to you on a dark, rainy, and gloomy day from Havana, Cuba. I so much miss the feel of your touch, the comfort of your arms around me, the soft connect of your lips with mine, but mostly the warmth of your heart. I realize and accept the fact that it is unlikely you will ever have the opportunity to read this or know how I feel, or what I have been thinking. I am living in an old abandoned boat I fixed up at Marina Hemmingway with the hopes and plans to somehow return to Florida. I thought I could stowaway or return as a guest of a Floridian tourist. I soon found out there are not many American tourists in Cuba legally yet. But I will not give up. If I have to swim the ninety miles across the ocean to see you, I will.

I want to be able to tell you face-to-face that I no longer blame you for our breakup or problems. As I said, Powell, the past months have given me much time to think about the life we once shared. Although it seems doubtful, I pray each day to have that life back. And Powell, I want so much to share it with you. I also realize I am writing this letter as much for myself as I am in the hopes of you reading it. As Sister Mary Elizabeth used to tell you in sixth-period class, "Confession is good for the soul."

Trying to recall and relive all of the horrible events that landed me here has been exhausting. Looking back at what started this nightmare has been a little cloudy. I remember checking myself into Seaman's Hospital in Key West. After our breakup, I could not eat. I lost fifteen pounds in ten days and became very tired and weak. I got so pale in the face I knew something was wrong. It was not until two weeks later when my lips turned blue, and I felt so dizzy I passed out and hit my head that I somehow drove myself to the hospital to find out what was going on.

The doctor said I was anemic and immediately administered iron and vitamin supplements intravenously in my arm. I was highly medicated for a few days and honestly was totally out of it. It was all a dream like I was asleep and able to hear but not consciously see what was occurring around me. Days later, a new doctor with a heavy Middle Eastern accent showed up and transported me to a large medical ship. The image of a huge red cross on the side of an enormous hellish rusty ship still lingers in my memory. The only thing I distinctly remember hearing at the time was that they seemed extremely enthusiastic about my rare blood type. The boat's medical staff kept me drugged to the point where I had no idea where I was or what was going on around me. I even had a dream I heard you and Limbo on the boat one time.

It was weeks later when I realized I had actually been kidnapped along with a few others and that we were headed to Cuba. There were two men and one other girl in the adjoining rooms. Their names were never mentioned, but the girl looked like she could have been my twin. When we first landed in Havana, I overheard enough conversation to realize what my fate was destined to be. All four of us had the same rare blood type, and we were about to unwillingly donate our vital organs. That is the moment I knew my life could be over, and that I would never see you again, Powell. I sobbed uncontrollably.

(Note to Self!) - Abdul Mutaar, Star of Ashrafi & Dr. Shezad.-

Powell, these are three names I am just now remembering. Obviously, I blocked this entire nightmare from my memory, but writing it all down on paper is bringing it back. Mutaar was the leader of the group who owned the ship, Star of Ashrafi, and was the brains behind the organ-trafficking business.

Dr. Shezad was the physician who would perform the surgeries. However, he was killed earlier before he was able to collect any organs from the four of us. Our organs were to be harvested in Cuba and transported by helicopter somewhere nearby. The recipient was a friend of Abdul Mutaar and the son of a very powerful important Muslim. I'm not sure why, but it may have been the Shah of Iran. However, I am not positive about that. It just popped into my head as the details are very blurry and there is a good possibility that I imagined that also. I was so drugged on that last night, everything is still very cloudy. And believe me, I have tried to recall every detail. I had relived those final hours over and over in hopes of finding answers and peace in my own mind.

One of my surprising recollections was that one of the men actually wanted to help us escape. He spoke very little English, but I got the impression he did not fully understand Mutaar's plans until too late. So much was going on, it all seems to run together now when I think about it. The helpful man grabbed me, ran down many flights of rusty stairs to an outside deck on the rear of the ship and threw me overboard. When I hit the frigid water, I immediately sobered up from the effects of the drugs. Things I remember include the sounds of a helicopter landing on the ship, total darkness in the cool water, the light pollution from a large city in the near distance, my rescuer running back into the ship to possibly rescue the others and lastly the sound of a fierce, intense explosion. I swam as fast and hard as I could towards the city lights as pieces of the shattering ship splashed the waters around me. Sadly I knew no one could have survived that extremely violent detonation. I would never be able to thank the man who had saved me. And only me!

When I finally reached the distant shore, I dragged myself up the steep jetty over very sharp barnacled rocks that sliced my body like a razor blade. The town was in a panic. . Red flashing lights from the police, fire trucks, and emergency vehicles swarmed the streets in a sudden stampede. There was utter panic and chaos. I was still naked, cold, and bleeding and looked as if I had been attacked by Jack the Ripper. I managed to stumble through the shadows of the Cuban streets unnoticed, trying to get as far away as possible. By morning, I had discovered what looked like a desolate, abandoned boat yard. Later, I re-

alized it was Marina Hemingway, the largest marina in all of Cuba. The sight of numerous battered billboards that surrounded the decaying concrete-laden harbor was intimidating to me. Huge photographs of Fidel Castro and Che Guevara, who once led the successful Cuban revolution stood tall, still screaming propaganda from a time past. "Revolution! Viva Cuba Libre! Socialism Muerte!"

Powell, I was more frightened and terrified than I thought possible. I mean really Powell, Socialism or Death? I know it is 2017 now and the U.S. is making progress with the Castro regime, but if caught, I feel strongly that I would be treated as the enemy. I am a refugee in a communist country. The papers here say a woman was seen jumping from the ship in Havana Harbor only minutes before an explosion destroyed it and everyone aboard. They say this woman is the one who planted the bomb. So you see, Powell, that is the reason I am hiding here. But my luck did take a turn for the better. Desperate and feeling completely hopeless, I approached a young Cuban taxi driver on the day after my escape. I was still naked, scared and badly injured from the barnacles. I felt as if I were at the end of my rope with nothing else to lose. Luckily the young cabbie Waldo, and his father Alexis were compassionate, caring people who understood the gravity of my unfortunate situation. Waldo gave me his shirt to wear, shielded me from the public eye and drove me to his family's home. Waldo is twenty-five years old, his sister is thirty, and lucky for me, they both speak very good English. His mom and dad only speak Spanish. The four years of Spanish I took in college is coming back to me quickly. They doctored me, clothed me, fed me, and made me feel like part of their family. I have found that the Cuban people are all nice, friendly, and happy. If not for Waldo and his family there is no telling what would have happened to me. I owe them my life. I work with Waldo's sister in a small motel outside of Havana where we clean the rooms, and I tend bar at night. I live on an abandoned boat that I fixed up that was once owned by Waldo's uncle. I make all of thirty dollars a month. The only thing that keeps me going Powell is the hopes of returning to Florida soon.

I have no access to telephones or computers. There is no mail service to the United States at all. The Cuban government controls the internet, and not even natives like Waldo are allowed to connect. Obviously, after Fidel's death, Raul does not want the Cuban people to know how the rest of the world lives. I do know that Waldo has relatives somewhere in South Florida. I will do whatever it takes to escape this island and see you again, Powell.

I hope that you get this letter somehow and know that I miss you, love you with all of my heart and want to put our lives back together.

I am forever yours

Dawn

CHAPTER 12

Hilda Tucker was a miserable woman. She was old, obnoxious, unattractive, and grossly obese. But this had not always been the case. Hilda was an attractive lady when she wore a younger woman's body. After many failed relationships due mainly to her recalcitrant need to always be in control, her life took a sudden turn for the worse. Hilda Tucker slipped into a deep depression that became terribly destructive. She became a bitter recluse, unable to function in a society she blamed for her problems. Hilda had never been socially accepted. Even with her earlier beauty, she seldom had more than one or two dates with the same man. It started off well but always ended abruptly. Her need to dominate, to be in charge of every situation, did not sit right with most guys. It was always her choice of restaurants, bars, movies, and even what friends to include. She was the master of subtle control. After each breakup or rejection, she would make up excuses or lies as to why it was always his fault. In time, Hilda blamed all men. They were just immature or selfish or too controlling themselves. When she was thirty-two years old, she decided maybe she was a lesbian and would experiment with girls. She soon discovered that most of the girls were as turned off by her commanding personality as the men were. Of course, it was not her fault. No man or woman could understand her. By the time she turned forty, the depression had taken its toll. She was an intolerable, foul, and negative woman who let herself sink to an insufferable low. At age seventy-two, her once beautiful, slim, curvaceous body, strawberry hair, and green eyes were now unrecognizable. Her thinning gray stringy mane hung low upon a massive round body. And over the years, her attitude had become as ugly and repulsive as her undisciplined, rotund carcass. The many souring years of unhappiness and stressful rejection turned Hilda into an unscrupulous, disgusting individual. What little joy she had in her life came from only two sources. First, from a local daily venomous blog she wrote, and secondly from her clever source of a very lucrative income. These were her only active hobbies.

Each morning, she logged in to Hilda's Blog Dot Biz to spew her vile, opinionated bullshit. As a former Key West councilwoman and self-proclaimed expert on any and all political issues, Hilda wrote paragraph after paragraph, in a literary style more suited to a third grader, that always fell on blind eyes and deaf ears. Her blog entries were similar to her early dates. People could only stomach one, maybe two at the most, before being repulsed. She was very lucky no one took her trash seriously. If they had, she most likely would have spent much of her time in court being sued for her lies and defamation of character. But Hilda never cared about the truth or doing the right thing. It was always all about her. Hilda Tucker was a wannabe her entire life. Writing her dishonest words in a blog gave her recognition, a forum, and the celebrity status that she so needed to stroke her ego. It did not matter nor did it ever occur to her that the attention was only in her own mind. As much happiness as writing her blog brought her, it was her second hobby that made her a wealthy woman.

The first occasion that it happened was an accident. It was nineteen years ago, late at night, after a few drinks in an Irish pub on Caroline Street in Old Town Key West. She wasn't paying attention when she missed a step, fell, and hit her head on the handrail. She was more embarrassed than hurt. But when the manager and many employees seemed so worried and concerned, she seized the opportunity. They settled for fifteen thousand dollars. After that memorable stumble, Hilda Tucker read up and studied all she could on the liability of "slip-and-fall" injury lawsuits. Over the years she became the clumsiest, most wealthy con in all of South Florida. Each circumstance was slightly different, but the outcome was always the same. She settled out of court. She had collected hundreds of thousands of dollars for such tragedies as "pain and suffering," lost wages, medical bills, loss of quality of life, negligence, and discrimination. But Hilda now had her eye on the big hit, the mother lode of all lawsuits, physical dis-figurement. After much more research, planning, and scheming, she had her plan. She needed a successful private business open to the public with high-end merchandise that required good insurance. It was her third day sitting in the rear of the conch train when the guide pointed out the very successful jewelry store on Duval Street.

"And if you look on the left side of the street you will notice Carib-bean Jewelry Company. They have six full-time bench jewelers and carry all of the finest brands in the jewelry business. If you need a Rolex watch, fine pearls, or a unique diamond engagement ring, Caribbean Jewelers is the place to go."

"Bingo!" Hilda thought, "I just hit the lottery again."

She was sure that she would soon be making a large cash deposit into her secure savings account at the Key West branch of South Beach Bank & Trust.

CHAPTER 13

Charlie's decision to cancel our planned fishing trip today turned out to be very good judgment on his part. Yesterday's gloomy weather forecast was uncommonly accurate. The unsettled waters in Garrison Bight where Charlie kept his new boat crashed against the bulkhead with an intense force. The forty-knot southwest wind was evidence of the forecast front blowing through. Limbo and I were not disappointed that today's trip had been postponed. Tomorrow's weather would be light winds and calm seas. Besides, Devin had called me late yesterday and left a message on my phone that Hilda Tucker and her attorney wanted to meet with me at the jewelry store around nine o'clock this morning. I was anxious to resolve this issue and hoped she would be reasonable. But the fact that she was bringing along her attorney gave me justifiable doubt. When I called Limbo to tell him that our fishing trip was rescheduled for tomorrow morning at seven o'clock, I also told him I was meeting the fat lady this morning. Before I hung up, he made me promise to fill him in after we had spoken.

As soon as I saw Hilda Tucker walk through the front door of the store, I knew I was in trouble. My hopes of resolving this reasonably were as far-fetched as the outfit the fat woman wore. Her hair was a shade of gray I'd not ever seen before. It was as if she had streaked it with green tints and mildew had begun to grow. Her sleeveless flowery muumuu exposed enormous flabby arms with faded tattoos from an era long gone. Her makeup was packed thick, her lips and marks on her teeth were a bright ruby red. The Kino's sandals on her bear-sized feet were as flattened and faded as a blown out truck tire. From each ear hung green and yellow four-inch long plastic earrings. But her most disturbing accessory was the discolored, washed out neck brace that hid her fourth chin, and it obviously had been used many times before today. Standing by Ms. Tucker's side with a briefcase in one hand and a business card in his other was the loathsome woman's attorney. And as disgusting as Hilda Tucker is, I had even less respect for him. It is bad enough for someone like the fat woman to be a con artist that preys on others for a profit, but for an attorney to do the same is downright criminal. I thought about threatening him with a frivolous lawsuit but decided to hold that card until later if needed.

After introductions, I escorted the hideous couple back to our private diamond room. We sat down, and I calmly asked, "Would you like something to drink before we get started?"

"No!" the attorney blurted out. "This is not a social call." He had a grotesque snarl on his face.

I bit my tongue trying not to respond negatively, hoping we could be civil. There was no sense in starting off on the wrong foot by allowing myself to be dragged down to his level. I refused to take the bait. I looked at Hilda until she made eye contact then I turned my focus to her attorney. I smiled and impulsively snapped, "Well if it's not a social call, what the hell is it, Matlock? You want to discuss your frivolous lawsuit?"

So much for holding back. I just could not help myself. Hilda suddenly turned a crimson red, not from embarrassment, but more like she was going to explode. I was about to ask if she was okay when her attorney screeched in my direction, "Matlock? Who the fuck are you calling Matlock?"

"Well if the seersucker suit fits, wear it!" I replied.

He started to say, "You assh—", when the fat woman started to cough, hiss, and retch as if having severe difficulty breathing. Her plump face turned from red to blue in seconds. Her lips were purple.

I'm thinking here comes another lawsuit. "Fat Woman Dies in Local Jewelry Store on Duval Street while in Diamond Room!"

Just then, Matlock reached over to the woman and ripped the Velcro on the back of the neck brace off as she and the brace hit the floor at the same instant. She fell on her right side gasping and sucking in air like a commercial vacuum cleaner. As the color started returning to her face, I was busy staring at her left arm. In faded ink was an alarming tattoo of a fat Elvis Presley holding what I hoped was a microphone up to his mouth. I was thinking Elvis probably gained weight as Hilda did when my thoughts were interrupted suddenly.

"I told you the brace was too damn tight!" the fat woman exclaimed.

Her attorney tried to shut her up. With his finger to his lips, he told her, "Shhh! Don't say anything else."

Hilda stood up, threw the brace across the room, knocking over an earring display on the sales floor while yelling, "I told you this wasn't going to work!"

As the fat woman and Matlock ran together towards the front door, he said, "See you in court."

I picked up the neck brace and Velcro piece off the floor to save for evidence in court. I also took a video of the attorney trying to catch up with the fat woman as she ran down the middle of Duval Street screaming at the top of her lungs, "You're fired, Matlock!"

However, I was confident that was not the end of Hilda Tucker.

CHAPTER 14

Limbo arrived at my back door a few minutes before six. The sun had not risen yet, and I was moving slowly. I managed to brew a pot of strong Café Bustelo before collecting my tackle and fly rods. By six-twenty, we were crossing the bridge from Summerland Key onto Little Torch. Once again, the forecast was accurate. With the sun just about to break through, the wind was slight and the seas were calm out over the ocean side as we drove across Niles Channel.

After a quick stop at Five Brothers Café, Limbo and I were on our way to meet Charlie in Key West. We both had a café con leche while waiting for Flora to make us their Cuban mix sandwiches for the boat. We arrived at Garrison Bight a few minutes before seven. We parked, and grabbed our gear and our ice chest full of beer, water, and food. We walked down the dock looking for Charlie's new boat. It was easy to spot, a brand new forty-five foot SeaVee with three oversized Yamaha outboards with *Heads Up* painted on the stern. How apropos, I thought to myself. With all the money he made from marketing a pill that cured erectile dysfunction the name was quite clever. Charlie was all smiles and chatter when we walked up.

"Come on aboard guys. We're all ready to go," he announced as he untied the dock lines from the cleats.

He slowly idled out between the markers taking us through the bight into the channel. Once clear of the no-wake zone, he jumped up on plane and headed west.

"Where we headed, Charlie?" I asked.

68

"It's a surprise, but I promise you will not only catch fish, but you will also love it," he replied.

Once we ran past the Marquesas, I knew we were on course to fish the Dry Tortugas. Over the past few years, while living in the Keys, Limbo and I have made this same trip, seventy miles west of Key West, many times. I have several memories of the Tortugas, some good and some dreadful. I saw no need to mention either to Charlie. Limbo glanced my way, raised one brow, and gave me a knowing smile. I suspected that he was remembering the same unpleasant trip I was. Names like Winston Sloan, Harrison Gray, and a go-fast boat called *Gold Digger* would never be discussed by either of us again. With over a thousand horsepower and calm seas, the seventy-mile trek from Key West to the Tortugas was quick and comfortable. When we passed Garden Key, one of the westernmost islands of the Florida Keys, I could see Fort Jefferson. A magnificent massive fortress built in 1847, it is the largest masonry structure in the western hemisphere. The fort is surrounded by a unique moat. It is also a famous bird and marine life sanctuary and is located on an island discovered by Ponce de Leon in 1513. And although it is rich in history with legends of pirates, sunken gold, and Dr. Samuel Mudd, I am most impressed for another reason. The more than sixteen million bricks used to build the fort were made a few miles from my hometown of Gulf Breeze, Florida. The Pensacola brickyard made the bricks and transported all sixteen million by sailing ship to the island.

Charlie anchored us up in sixty feet of water, easily in view of Garden and Loggerhead Keys. I was surprised to see that Charlie was so well-prepared and so knowledgeable with his fishing skills. With plenty of live bait along with a very impressive chum line, it only took a few minutes for the fish to show up. Limbo landed the first two nice fish. The black grouper weighed forty-nine pounds, and his mutton snapper tipped the scales at nineteen pounds. Both were enviable catches. For the next hour, I patiently waited with my fly rods hoping yellowfin tuna or wahoo would show up on the surface in the chum line. Meanwhile, Charlie and Limbo filled the ice chest with an assortment of great eating fish. From flag-sized yellowtail snapper, black and red grouper, and mutton snapper to huge red snapper, all were impressive.

I saw some surface activity behind the boat within casting distance. Guessing from the size of the splashes, I assumed it was wahoo, not tuna. I picked up the fly rod with a large six-inch white deceiver fly and a wire leader. As I began to false cast the pilchard-like fly towards the surface strikes Charlie said, "Hey Powell, I looked into Hilda's background."

"Hilda?" I questioned.

"Yeah, the fat lady who fell in your store."

I knew who he meant, I just wanted him to think it was not important enough for me to be concerned. Which was not true at all of course. I picked up the fly, double hauled a couple of false casts and shot the fly out about ninety feet behind the boat. I stripped the fly in with very fast short strips making the fly swim and dance like a wounded pilcher.

"This isn't the first time she slipped and fell in a business," Charlie continued with a satisfied look of pride in his eyes.

I continued to cast and strip the fly in as if not to pay attention. I heard Limbo ask Charlie something out of my ears' reach. I was quite sure that Captain Limbo had already used his sources to investigate Hilda Tucker's fraudulent past. But I was hoping we may learn even more from Charlie's insatiable hunger for gossip. I would retrieve this newly learned knowledge from Limbo later tonight as we enjoyed a feast of fresh fried grouper and snapper ceviche on my back deck.

Seeing two simultaneous splashes on the surface sixty feet back, with one back cast I laid the fly between them. Bullseye! The water exploded. My fly line jumped, and the fly reel screeched and hissed, spinning out of control when the hooked wahoo leaped six feet in the air. Within seconds, the wahoo's blistering speed of over sixty miles per hour had stripped off two hundred or more yards of backing. Without the wire leader attached to the fly, his razor sharp teeth would have sliced through a normal line the second he hit.

I put as much pressure on the fish as I felt the twenty-pound tippet could take. I needed to hear more about what Charlie had to say about Hilda Tucker, but I did not want to lose this fish. From the size of the flashes under the surface along with his speed, I knew this fish was over sixty pounds, a personal record for me on fly. So I decided to fight the fish and talk with Charlie later. The fish was a beast. For each foot I would retrieve, he would pull out two more. This unpredictable tug of war between fish and man was brutal. After battling twenty-five minutes, he made his last very impressive run. At top speed, the wahoo sliced through the waters throwing a rooster tail wake a foot high into the air as the fly reel spun in reverse so rapidly that it created a small cyclonic water spout in my hand.

Realizing what a nice fish this was, Limbo and Charlie had joined me at the stern of the boat cheering me on with sincere enthusiasm. I was finally able to recover all of the four hundred yards of backing along with the hundred feet of fly line and bring the monster-sized fish to the boat. Charlie had grabbed the gaff, and with one swift movement he stuck the fish and yanked him into the boat. The beautiful rich blue bands on the fish's silvery sides lit up like a neon Greek flag. Immediately following the high fives, in an attempt to remind us how the fish came upon its unique name, Limbo screamed out, "WAHOO!"

After taking too many photos, we measured the fish to be fifty-nine inches long. With some magical mathematical formula, Limbo estimated the fish to weigh forty-nine pounds. It had taken me an hour to land. The ride back to Key West was quick, comfortable, and uneventful. Once we reached the docks, Limbo and I cleaned the fish while Charlie washed down his new fishing machine.

Anxious to quiz Charlie for information on the fat lady, I invited him over to have dinner with Limbo and me. He quickly accepted.

CHAPTER 15

Limbo arrived at my home with a twelve-pack of Landshark thirty minutes before Charlie arrived. This gave the two of us enough time to prepare for dinner and to devise a plan to get information out of Charlie without looking too obvious. After a very long day on the water, it felt good to sit back and relax for a few moments once we finished prepping. Talking with Limbo, I immediately realized that he was as unsure and distrusting of Charlie than I was, or maybe even more so.

I attributed my doubt and suspicions to Charlie's personality. I felt that his loud, flamboyant, and overly confident personality was the result of his successful marketing mind and business achievement, along with the fact that he was a self-made millionaire that ran in elite circles with the pretty, the rich, and the famous. Charlie's arrival to my driveway did not disappoint. With the sounds of screeching tires, honking horns, and loud music blasting from within the lush interior, Charlie made a spectacular entrance. But I would have expected nothing less.

He called us outside to give us his best salesman's pitch of his Jaguar XJR with a 5.0 liter V8 550HP supercharged engine. He pronounced the car's name in an impressive but distorted British accent. What I thought was a two-syllable exotic auto name, he was able to transform into three syllables. It was a beautiful car with a fine finish, great detail, and a luxurious interior of piano black wood veneer and jet black leather. I was especially impressed with the umbrella holder in the trunk. After Charlie finished his description of the car he, as I suspected he would, shared with us the price.

"You can't believe the deal I got. It lists for one forty-nine five, but I stole it for a hundred and twenty-nine thousand six hundred and fifty dollars."

Although somewhat ostentatious, Charlie's arrogance and pomposity are not offensive. It's almost as if he is portraying a character in a well-cast movie. However, had he bought that eight-carat diamond ring from my competitor, I probably would think differently. I can hold a grudge, and I will not deny that fact. But he didn't buy it elsewhere. I love Charles Switzer, at least for now, despite lingering suspicions.

With a brisk south wind blowing across Cudjoe Bay tonight, I thought it best to eat inside. Although the back deck is much more to my liking, I did not feel like trying to explain the smell of monkey manure to Sir Charles. Limbo grabbed us a couple of beers from the ice chest and asked Charlie what he would like. Before he could reply Limbo said, "We don't have mint for mojitos."

Charlie smiled and asked, "You have any scotch?"

I nodded to Limbo and pointed to the liquor cabinet.

Normally I would season, score, and deep fry the yellowtail snapper whole and serve with beans and rice. But tonight I wanted to be able to sit and talk with Charlie. I picked a less demanding recipe this night. I had already seasoned a few mutton snapper fillets with lime juice, salt, pepper, and garlic powder. I dredged them in flour in a Ziploc bag. I also had peeled two large very ripe mangos, saving all the syrup. When Limbo's saffron rice was ten minutes from done, I heated olive oil in a large skillet. I sautéed all three of the fillets until nice and brown on both sides. I added a little butter to the pan and placed the mangos on top of the fish pouring the syrup over it all. I covered the skillet and let it simmer until Limbo's rice was ready. The "Mango Snapper" recipe was given to me by a local fishing guide who became a dear friend over the years. José Wejebe went on to be quite a celebrity in the world of fishing. In the early years, he guided many fishermen to world-record fish and many great days on the waters. Later, he traveled the world fishing and filming his adventures for his television show, *The Spanish Fly*, which he named after his boat. The last time I saw José, we shared a great meal together at the Square Grouper

Bar and Grill. We talked, laughed, and reminisced for hours reliving our many escapades together on his boat fishing. Three days after that José was killed in a plane crash while fishing in the Everglades. And tonight's meal would remind me just how much I missed my Cuban friend.

While enjoying a Keys feast of fresh fish and Cuban rice, we dined inside, which was, without a doubt, the right choice. We were able to see the light of the moon over Cudjoe Bay but without the foul smell of monkey feces lingering in the air.

As if right on cue, Limbo started his relaxed interview. "So Charlie, don't you work at the Key West branch of South Beach Bank?"

"Not exactly," Charlie replied, "I am on the board of the bank. The main location is in Miami, but we have a satellite branch here in Key West."

"Do you enjoy it?" Limbo questioned.

"Oh yes, very much. It is a very high-tech, state-of-the-art banking operation and does very well. I've met plenty of great people through the bank, and I am able to help businesses and individuals with loans or many other financial needs. And not to mention, I have access to an extreme amount of confidential information on most everyone who banks with us."

Limbo glanced over at me as to say, "You take it from here."

I did just that.

"So, I guess Charlie, that article I read a few weeks back about five million dollars missing from a dead man's account didn't hurt the bank's PR?" I quizzed.

"Well, I have to admit, that was a tricky one for sure, but the bank came out fine," Charlie replied.

"But what about the five million dollars? What happened with that?" I asked.

"After internal and outside investigations, it was determined that it had to be a family member who transferred the money. In fact, we assumed the deceased man did it just hours before his death."

"But the article said it was stolen after the man's death," I said.

"Well, that would be impossible," Charlie assured. "He had the new fingerprint scan program set up to all of his accounts, so the only person that could have accessed them was him. No one can fake his fingerprint you know, and no two prints are alike. In any case, the insurance company settled with the widow."

Something just did not sound right in Charlie's voice. He wasn't his usual sure and confident self. He was passive, calculating, and focused on his words.

So I asked him, "Do many people have the fingerprint scanning program for banking access? Do you think it is safe and foolproof?"

"Oh yes, for sure!" he snapped. "It's the best there is. All new customers in the bank have it. In fact, that is how I got all of the information on Hilda Tucker, the fat lady that is going to sue you."

I saw a subtle smile on Limbo's face as he probably noticed one on mine. Charlie just saved us the trouble of trying to bring up the fat lady in conversation.

"Sue me?" What are you talking about? No one ever mentioned lawsuits, Charlie!"

That's when Charlie Switzer returned to his comfortable, confident, and charismatic self.

"This will be her ninth slip-and-fall lawsuit in ten years. And she has settled out of court on every one of them," Charlie said. "And although the insurance companies know that Hilda the Hun's big ass is a con artist, it is impossible to prove. In every case, they settle early just to shut her up. Bad publicity is not something anyone wants to deal with. And I'm sure you are no different, Powell," Charlie continued.

I acted shocked and upset at the news, trying not to let Charlie know I had already spoken with Hilda.

"Yes, Charlie, you are right. The last thing I need is bad publicity or people thinking the store is unsafe. I've worked too hard to let someone ruin our reputation. I surely hope you are wrong about her, but in the meantime, I'll call her to meet me and try to see what she wants," I said with a straight face.

"I'd give it a couple of days before you call. Maybe she'll change her mind or just go away, disappear even. You never know!" Charlie uttered.

I felt Limbo's stare on the back of my neck. I'm sure Charlie's message was as disturbing for Limbo as it was for me. It was not so much what Charlie said as how he said it and the evil look in his eye at the time.

CHAPTER 16

Dark, angry clouds filled the sky above raging seas that spun uncontrollably from every direction. The ocean turbulence had no direction, no focus but only a disorderly, vehement tidal flow. Today's weather conditions were as out of control as Charlie Switzer himself. A rational thinker and an intelligent man, in spite of his own behavior, Charlie knew right from wrong. And his obsession with just how wrong it was of Hilda to extort his new friend Powell dominated his every thought. He could not let her get away with yet another unethical trick. He had to do something. He had to stop her. He must teach Hilda, the fat lady, a lesson. It was the right thing to do. At least that was what he told himself in order to rationalize what he had planned and why.

Charlie crafted a carefully thought out plan as if he were presenting an important marketing proposal to a client. With his connections at the bank, he researched Hilda Tucker thoroughly. In her file, he had assembled everything from recent photographs, addresses, phone numbers, hobbies and emails to bank account numbers, and which finger she scanned to access them all. Reading through her file made Charlie smile. Charlie found the newspaper clipping of Hilda on a lower Keys bird watching tour especially interesting. That was the moment his plan came together.

When Hilda's phone rang, she assumed it was either her attorney or an annoying solicitor calling. No one called "Hilda the Hun" these days, not even her own family. Her disgusting attitude and personality had run everyone off. How she longed for the days when she enjoyed a man's companionship.

"Hello, who is this?" she barked into the phone.

"Hi, Miss Tucker. This is Charlie Switzer with your bank downtown on Duval Street. I have some great news for you," he said.

"Yeah? What the hell you selling, Mr. Sweitzer?" she blurted back.

"It's Switzer, not Sweitzer, Miss Tucker and I'm not selling anything. You won a raffle drawing out of all our customers for a guided eco tour and birding trip to the Dry Tortugas. It is an all-day trip and includes lunch and drinks," Charlie replied.

Hilda thought about it for a minute, let it sink in, and actually answered with joy in her voice for the first time in a while.

"Really, Mr. Switzer? That's great, I've always wanted to go birding in the Dry Tortugas. I read that some great birds nest over there, some I don't have on my life list yet. How soon can we go?"

"Is tomorrow too soon?" Charlie asked.

Hilda Tucker was ecstatic and agreed to meet Charlie at his boat *Heads Up* at five o'clock first thing in the morning. It would still be pitch dark outside for their departure, which of course was the plan for a reason.

After dinner, she packed her day bag with binoculars, bird books, checklist, cameras, and sunscreen. When Hilda finally laid her head on the pillow, she could not help but think how happy she was. Soon she would collect more money than she could possibly spend from a local Key West jewelry store, and tomorrow she would enjoy a trip she had only imagined. Life was good, and she fell asleep dreaming of a long life of pleasure with plenty of money. But Hilda had no idea of just how wrong she was.

Morning came quickly. Hilda jumped up and couldn't help smiling as she prepared herself a mammoth breakfast. She then dressed and hurried to Garrison Bight Marina to meet her guide and banker Charlie Switzer. The sun had just begun to rise off the bow as they headed west. What Hilda Tucker never suspected was that it would be a one-way ride.

CHAPTER 17

Captain Limbo is six foot from his bare feet to the top of his shaved scalp. The man is two hundred pounds of weathered fitness, friendliness, and too many scars to count. His almost clumsy gait resembles the stealth of a blue heron stalking its prey in shallow waters. Over the past few years, Limbo and Powell had become very good friends. They had shared many magical times but also many scary and dark times as well. One of the most tragic happened only last year. Although Limbo was now retired from the U.S. Customs Office, he still had many friends in the Key West office on Roosevelt Boulevard. So, when his cell phone rang, he was not overly surprised to hear a friendly voice from the past.

"Hey Limbo, it's Bob Papp. How are you doing?"

"I'm great, Admiral but what do I owe this unexpected pleasure? It's not every day the commandant of the Coast Guard calls," Limbo said.

"Well pal, I'm not calling today as Admiral Papp, I'm calling as your friend Bob."

Still anchored off of Key West Harbor, Limbo leaned back in his seat up on the bow of his boat to listen to what Admiral Robert Papp had to say. It was a remarkable story that brought Limbo to tears, tears of joy.

Bob Papp began by saying, "Limbo, do not say a word. Just listen to what I have to say and remember I know you were in Cuba last year and I know why. You and I spoke many times about your friend Powell Taylor and Dawn Landry. I wish I could have been more help but Cuba was a different country a year ago."

"What are you getting at Bob?" Limbo interrupted.

"What I'm getting at is some very good news for your friend Powell. Dawn is still very much alive and well."

"What? Are you sure?" Limbo exclaimed.

"Yes, Limbo, I am. Let me explain."

Captain Limbo listened with stunned silence as Admiral Bob Papp explained. "A letter written by Dawn to Powell came into our possession last week. I didn't call because I wanted to make sure it was legit before I got your hopes up."

"Are you sure it was written by Dawn?" Limbo said.

"Yes, one hundred percent yes," the Admiral replied.

And then Admiral Papp read Dawn's letter to Limbo. It convinced him that she truly did pen the words. Bob Papp did not know all of the details of what happened that night a year ago in Havana and did not want to know. He knew his friend Limbo was involved, there was an explosion on a ship where many people died. That was all he had to know.

"Where is Dawn now?" Limbo asked.

"She is still in Cuba as she said in the letter. Although Cuba and the United States are moving towards normalization of relations for the first time in fifty years, it will take some time before the U.S. removes its commercial, economic, and financial embargo. And it is not possible for anyone to travel between the two countries easily unless you have family in Cuba."

"Well, how did you get the letter then?" Limbo interrupted again.

"Her friend Waldo in Havana finally was cleared to visit his relatives in South Florida. Dawn gave him the letter to try and find Powell. When he cleared customs, they found the letter, and they immediately contacted me."

Admiral Papp explained to Limbo that the Cuban government was still investigating the explosion of the ship that Dawn had escaped from and it was not safe for her to try and leave yet.

Limbo's brain was spinning, trying to figure a way to get Dawn back. He decided not to mention anything to Powell yet. There was no sense in getting his hopes up until it was confirmed.

"Does Dawn know you have the letter?" Limbo asked.

"Yes, Waldo and his sister in Cuba communicate weekly. He told her that U.S. Customs took the letter. That is all she knows," Bob answered.

Limbo was torn on what to do. Should he tell Powell? Or should he just figure a way to get a boat to Havana and bring her home?

"Bob, if I get a boat can you help me get Dawn back to the States?" Limbo asked.

"All I can do is get you clearance into Havana and back into Florida. The rest is up to you. And frankly the less I know, the better," Bob replied.

Limbo thanked his friend and asked him to mail a copy of the letter along with the proper paperwork to get him access to Marina Hemingway in Havana to his post office box on Summerland Key.

After he hung up with the Admiral, Limbo had a brainstorm of an idea. Who did he know with a big enough boat to easily get to Cuba fast? And who had a boat and a huge ego and wanted desperately to help his new friend Powell Taylor?

Besides, Limbo wanted to talk with him and discuss a few things, such as fat Hilda and his obsession to help Powell. Sir Charles Switzer should expect a call from me soon, he thought.

Charlie Switzer was most thrilled when his cell phone rang, and he immediately recognized Captain Limbo's voice. However, it was not an easy phone call for Limbo to make. He had tried to think of every possibility there was to rescue Dawn from Havana. He even began to question if it were logical or possible she really was still alive. But he knew that if Admiral Papp said she was alive and well that it had to be true. But still, just in case it wasn't, or on the chance something went wrong, Limbo decided not to tell Powell of his plans. He had already made one mistake when he lied and told his friend that he had seen Dawn's dead body that night on the ship.

"Charlie, I need a huge favor if possible," Limbo whispered into the phone.

"Sure, Limbo, anything you need," Sir Charles answered.

Limbo told Charlie the entire story of Dawn's disappearance, the organ thieves, and the demonic-looking ship that landed in Havana last year with a drugged Dawn Landry. He went on to tell how she had been kidnapped for her organs because of her rare blood type that matches the Shah of Iran's only son. He also confessed to Charlie that in all of the confusion and fear of not getting off that ship before it exploded, he told Powell that he had seen Dawn's dead body. It turned out that it was not Dawn at all, but another poor, unfortunate girl who could have been her twin.

"So that is why I do not want Powell to know what we are planning."

Limbo left out many of the details before and after the explosion, and the night it occurred in Havana Harbor. Limbo still was not sure if he could totally trust Charlie. He wanted to like him and trust him, but he was not yet convinced. Right now, however, he had no choice.

Charlie's sudden feeling of excitement and pleasure was obvious to Limbo when he asked him, "Would you mind taking me to Marina Hemingway in Havana Cuba on your new boat?"

In fact, he was so excited, Limbo thought he could almost feel a crazed look in Charlie's eyes when he replied, "Hell no, I don't mind Limbo, you just made my day. And I cannot wait to get to know each other better. How soon can we leave?"

"Is next week too soon?" Limbo asked.

"Not at all pal," Charlie answered.

Limbo was up most of the next four nights worrying that he had made a huge mistake, thinking maybe he should keep his distance with this Charlie Switzer. There were too many weird coincidences that seem to surround Charlie. His obsession with huge Hilda, his position of board member on the bank, missing monies, security bypassing, and his mysterious behavior and personality were just a few. Before Limbo was able to close his eyes and fall asleep, he convinced himself he was just paranoid. Charlie is a good guy to help me out on such short notice, he thought. And yet the doubt persisted.

Limbo was up early, packed a small duffel bag for the trip, brewed a pot of coffee and made a couple of phone calls. He knew Powell would be up this time of day but was surprised when Admiral Bob Papp answered his cell phone. Limbo told Powell that he would be gone a day or two next week but would get together when he returned.

"So where you going this time, Limbo? Find another sun bunny tourist to sail to the Marquesas with you?" Powell asked.

"Something like that. I'll see you in a few," Limbo responded.

It was not uncommon for Limbo to disappear for a few days or weeks even. So, Powell was not alarmed or curious in any way. It was just another one of Limbo's booty cruises.

His conversation with the Admiral was much more important. His friend Bob Papp gave him all of the GPS coordinates necessary to navigate into Havana Harbor and through the narrow inlet to Marina Hemingway. He also had a list of names of people who could help him locate Dawn if it became necessary. He described the boat and its location where Dawn was living or more accurately, hiding.

"She's always back there by six o'clock, Limbo. She is not expecting you because I told no one. I did not want to take any risks that might endanger Dawn."

Limbo thanked his friend and hung up.

Limbo finished his cup of coffee, checked his anchor, and lowered his dinghy into the water. He smiled thinking how nice it was to have a boat in Key West. Although no sun was visible, beautiful sunlight lit up the sky, and there was no traffic.

"Does not get any better than this," Limbo thought.

CHAPTER 18

Before meeting Charlie at his boat this morning, Hilda prepared herself a magnificent breakfast. Today she was celebrating two of her only joys left in life, eating and bird watching.

Once again Charlie Switzer's uncanny ability to read a person's inner thoughts was right on target. That was just one more reason for his financial success. He knew offering her a birding adventure was the only way to get her offshore.

Hilda arose with rare excitement today, two hours early so to enjoy her monumental meal. Hilda's four-egg omelet was a masterpiece. She first fried the bacon and pork sausage in lard she had purchased at Fausto's Cuban grocery in old town Key West a couple days earlier. The fresh yard eggs were from a neighbor who let their chickens roam free in the streets. Hilda added cheddar cheese, mushrooms, and red onion with the bacon and pork. She then fried the egg omelet with some potatoes in the lard with the rendered bacon and pork fat. As she was pouring a large glass of chocolate milk, the timer on the oven sounded. "Perfect timing," she thought to herself. The large cathead buttermilk biscuits were drenched in butter and Nutella before she added them to her plate. Hilda was more than pleased with the enormous platter of food she now stared at, salivating as if it would be her last meal. Which of course it would be.

Hilda knew that eating like this was not only unhealthy but was also the reason she looked like she did. She did not care about her looks or her life anymore. Her vanity disappeared with her youth and her beauty many years ago. Besides if she were thin and beautiful her "slip-and-fall" schemes would never work, or for that matter, be necessary.

When Hilda arrived at Garrison Bight Marina promptly on time, *Heads Up* was purring like a kitten and ready to go. When she stepped aboard, the gunwale creaked and cracked from the weight of her porcine body. For a slight moment, she pondered a "slip-and-fall" incident. But not today. Nothing would spoil her birding trip to the Tortugas, not even greed. Although from the looks of Charlie's boat, her banker might be on the list for a later date.

As Charlie grabbed her arm to help her aboard he was almost positive he smelled bacon. The stench that surrounded Hilda's body like a halo was not only nauseating, it drew flies to her like a dog's ass in the heat of summer. Some were even trapped in her foul green nappy hair. Charlie almost gagged when he realized the swine-like smells were being emitted from the pores of this porker, Hilda Tucker. In a morbid way, it was a relief for Charlie that she was so vile. Had she been pleasant, thin and beautiful he would never be able to carry out his plan. A plan that would help his new friend, Powell Taylor, and would not only save his reputation but also his jewelry store. At least that is what he kept telling himself. It was a rationalization that eased Charlie's guilt for what he had to do.

Luckily the wind was light, and the trip to the Tortugas was quick and easy. By the time *Heads Up* pulled into Garden Key in the Dry Tortugas, Hilda had organized all of her birding gear. She unpacked binoculars, bird book, and bird list for the Lower Keys and Dry Tortugas, a pen, a yellow marker, two bags of Doritos, and three bags of Cheetos. Her backpack looked more like a self-made lunchbox packed by a preadolescent schoolkid.

Although in Charlie Switzer's past, he had carried out a few misdeeds which included not only unethical behavior but also illegal criminal acts, he had never committed murder. To most people, this would be a problem, but absolutely not for Sir Charles. He, through his own justification, had convinced himself it was the right and only choice he had. This horrid woman Hilda had to be stopped. He could not let her continue her newest dishonest profession and ruin his dear friend, Powell Taylor. But then again, it was only in his own delusional mind that he and Powell were close friends, or even friends at all. Besides, Charlie had an even better reason to terminate

Hilda the Horrible.

Charlie was an analytical thinker who always faced every project with a calm, intelligent, and deductive approach. And with this project, a cold-blooded murder of a pathetic old woman, his path to success could be no different. Charlie read, studied, thought deeply, and drew out every scenario his tainted mind could imagine for the perfect murder at sea. Earlier he had made a list, writing it down so he could study each plot, think it out, and deduce a rational plan of action.

As Charlie idled the boat between Garden and Bush Keys, he pointed out to Hilda the many terns and noddies nesting on the shore of Bush Key. He then removed his list from his back pocket to review his notes one last time. Looking over the top of his sunglasses he smiled when he read number seven on his presentation.

Ways The Ocean Can Kill You
by
Charles Switzer

1. Drowning.

Although probably the most obvious and most likely way to die in the ocean I doubt I could get Hilda in a swim suit. And if I did, there is no way I could hold her big ass under long enough to fill her gargantuan lungs with saltwater. There is a good chance that not only would there be signs of a struggle on her body but also on mine. And that's if she didn't drown me first. SO, NO!

2. Capsizing/Propeller Cuts.

Although my research shows two hundred and sixty people a year drown from boats capsizing, I really don't want to sink my boat. But the prop cuts are a possibility.

3. Boat Explosion.

Two hundred fifty boats explode every year in the United States. But again, I want to keep *Heads Up*. So, No!

4. Diving Accident.

The Tortugas would be the perfect setting for such an easy to get away with murder. I could get Hilda down about one hundred feet and pick my method; running out of air (I'm sure she would suck the air out of a tank immediately), equipment malfunction, stuck in the coral, or sucked away in a current. But then I'm back to the same problem, getting Hilda in a suit and willing to dive. So, No!

5. Hypothermia.

No way will that work. Who's going to believe Hilda's mass died of hypothermia when the water temp must be ninety degrees. No!

6. Getting Lost at Sea.

Possible, I think. I could navigate off course south of the Tortugas knock her in the head and dump her overboard. No, even if I could somehow pick her limp large body up high enough to toss over the gunwale, with my luck some sailboat would spot her a mile away, floating on the surface like a wounded whale. No!

7. Fishing Accident.

Now, this has potential, especially if I combine it with part of option #2.

"Captain" Charlie shoved the wrinkled kill list into his front pocket as he, with so much charisma, continued with the tour.

"Hilda honey, if you look out to the left on Garden Key you will see Fort Jefferson. This is where Confederate war prisoners were held during the Civil War. This is also the only Key in the Dry Tortugas where people are allowed to camp."

"You don't have to worry about my fat ass ever seeing the inside of a tent Charlie," she replied with a grotesque grin. "I hate bugs, and if you haven't noticed, I sweat a lot."

Charlie nodded and said, "On the right is Bush Key, known for many nesting sea birds. It was originally called Hog Island because pigs were raised there to feed the prisoners at Fort Jefferson."

Hilda turned and yelled, "Charlie," until he looked at her eye to eye. She lifted up her sunglasses and said, "I love pork!" as she winked at him.

Charlie wanted to vomit as Hilda continued her flirtatious moves. But being the ultimate salesman, Charlie made her feel not only comfortable but beautiful too.

After many hours of watching rare birds that included frigates, boobies, tropicbirds, terns, gulls, and even some migrating warblers it was time to head back to Key West.

"The wind has kicked up a little, so the ride home will be a little slow. Would you like to fish on the way back?"

"I don't like to fish," Hilda said.

"Oh shit," Charlie thought. "What am I going to do?" But then, he immediately knew what to say.

"Oh Hilda, we are in luck, yellowfin tuna are biting. Have you ever tasted freshly caught tuna?"

"I love tuna, Charlie. Let's give it a try."

"Sure, but let's only keep a few. I'll clean them when we get back to the docks. Are you in a big hurry to get back? Is anyone expecting you?" Charlie asked.

"Oh, hell no, captain. I'm all yours. In fact, nobody even knows I'm out here."

With that music to his ears, Charlie pulled out a couple of rods, cast them out, and stuck them in rod holders on either side of the stern. He then took out his phone and hit video.

"Get ready Hilda, as soon as the big one hits I'm gonna get you on tape reeling him in."

Charlie pulled the typed list from his pocket one last time. He read number seven quickly again for inspiration before ripping it up and tossing it in the wake. But watching the paper get sucked into the propeller and then shredding it like a blender he couldn't shake one morbid but somewhat humorous thought.

"It ain't over till the fat lady sinks."

By the time Charlie idled into his boat slip at Garrison Bight, the sun had long set. This was not by accident either. It had been a long day but very eventful and immensely satisfying. A few people walked in the shadows of the dock lights as Charlie washed down his boat and unloaded all of his gear.

He opened up the trunk of his prized Jaguar and tossed in his backpack, camera, rods, reels, tackle box, and a small ice chest with three beers, a Diet Coke, and two human thumbs.

CHAPTER 19

Personal demons swirled uncontrollably in my dreams all night. Crazy thoughts and nightmares that seemed so believable in the dark made no sense now that it was light outside. Limbo's revelation about Dawn made me hopeful but anxious. Hilda the con artist wants to hurt my business and reputation, all in the name of raw greed. My new acquaintance, Charles Switzer, wants to be my new BFF. I shared Charlie's feelings about Hilda but found them very alarming. I spent much of the night trying to recall his exact words. "Maybe she will just go away, disappear even. You never know." I'm pretty sure I remember that accurately. Yes! I'm positive. That is exactly what he said and with conviction.

I was moving slowly but knew the caffeine in a strong cup of coffee would help. I sat on the back deck looking out on Cudjoe Bay. It was a beautiful morning. The sun was hot, big white puffy clouds floated towards the north, and a stiff southeast wind tickled the palm fronds bringing with it the slight familiar stench of monkey shit from Key Lois. By now I was so accustomed to the odor, I feared I was beginning to like it. Frigate birds circled above. Two immature white ibis were poking around in the grass near shore, and a huge, bright-green-colored iguana was sunning himself from the poling platform on my skiff. It was a Keys moment that made me realize once again just why I love it here.

Unfortunately, the feeling dissipated quickly. I knew I had phone calls to make, questions to answer, and problems to solve. I made another cup of Bustelo, sat down with my phone, and tackled my day.

I dialed Limbo first. His damn phone rang and rang with no answer. His voice mail was turned off. I would try back later.

Next, I called the jewelry store and asked Devin if she had heard any news from Hilda Tucker.

"No, not a word. Not since she stormed out of here the other day."

"Really?" I said. "That doesn't make sense. I'm pretty sure her threats to sue were real. Look up her phone number on the computer for me and grab her attorney's business card from my desk. I need his number also."

I waited a few minutes before Devin returned back to the phone and whispered in a low voice, "Okay, here's the fat fuck's number and her asshole lawyer's also!" she laughed, said goodbye, and hung up.

Devin was a great loyal employee, but for the life of me, I did not understand the mouth on her. Customers, however, love her and fortunately, she does indeed manage to tone down her offensive, distasteful language while working.

I dialed Hilda Tucker's number. A recorded message told me her phone was no longer in service. I thought that was odd. She would most definitely need a phone to make all of the necessary arrangements with attorneys, accountants, and doctors in order to sue me.

Next, I called Hilda's attorney who had accompanied her to my store. According to his business card, Matlock's real name was Terrence C. Capstone. After two transfers, Terry finally answered the call.

"Hello, Mr. Capstone. This is Powell Taylor from Caribbean Jewelry Company. I'm trying to get in touch with your client, Hilda Tucker, and discuss this fall."

"So, now I'm Mr. Capstone? What happened to Matlock? Oh never mind," he snapped before I could respond. "I don't have a clue where the fat fraud is," he continued. "In fact, if she didn't still owe me twenty-five hundred dollars, I would never want to see her big ole self ever again."

"Why is that?" I asked.

"The bitch fired me after we left your store."

Although that did not surprise me, after witnessing what took place between them that day.

I continued, "Do you know how to reach her? Her phone has been disconnected."

"Yes, I know that Mr. Taylor, I've been calling for a week now. It went dead three days ago."

"Do you have her address?" I asked.

"It won't do you any good. I drove by trying to catch her at home to get a payment day before yesterday. She's gone, moved out totally."

I thanked Matlock and said goodbye. As strange as it sounded, I hoped it was true, but I was confident I would probably hear from her new attorney with a whole new list of demands.

My last call of the day was the one I dreaded most. My new friend Charlie Switzer was exuberant when he answered.

"How you doing, Powell? I was just thinking about you the other day," Charlie exclaimed.

"I'm fine, Charlie. Thanks. Why were you thinking of me?" I asked.

"Well, actually I was going to call you tonight about that. I got your cell number from your bank account. Hope you don't mind, but I thought you would want to hear the good news."

"What news is that?" I blurted back.

"You remember Hilda Tucker, the fat woman who fell in your store, right? Well, we had a bank board meeting this morning, and it seems that yesterday afternoon Hilda closed out all of her accounts. She transferred all of her money to some offshore bank in Panama."

"Did she tell the teller why she was closing accounts?" I asked

"She didn't see a teller. She passed the security scan and sat down at our customer service desk and did the entire transfer on a computer. All three hundred twenty-six thousand dollars that her fat ass probably got from her bullshit slip-and-fall schemes. But the good news is, she won't be bothering you anymore. She's gone for good."

"How do you know that Charlie?" I asked with concern.

"Nobody would get through the fingerprint scan and transfer all their money if they weren't planning on leaving town for good."

I should have felt relief that Hilda Tucker possibly was gone and hopefully, no longer a threat. When I hung up the phone, I sensed something was wrong. I would have to wait and see if she contacted me again.

CHAPTER 20

It had been a magnificent day in the lower Keys, another in a picture perfect week for the many tourists that visited in search of catching a prized trophy for their wall.

By four o'clock in the afternoon, when Captain Rush Maltz idled his center console up to the docks at Murray's Marina, he had an ice chest full of world-class snapper and grouper. His charter group had driven down US 1 from Maine, and now their ivory white skin was scorched by the sun and yet they were all grins. The marina was busy with boats of all sizes and shapes motoring in and out. Flats skiffs were returning with their anglers after a day of chasing tarpon with fly rods. Offshore boats returned flying billfish flags that represented their released catches for the day. Other fisherman lined up to get photos beneath the marina's sign where their catch hung on nails baking in the sun's heat. Kneeling below their proud catch the sign above read in big bold letters,

"Caught out of Murray's Marina Stock Island in the Florida Keys."

The more photos taken here, the better it was for business. Dolphin watching catamarans were leaving the dock in search of playful porpoise that seemed to enjoy the annoying tourists that yelled, photographed, and tried to touch their favorite ocean mammals if they came close to the boat's side. But on this day, Captain Rush's thirty-two foot Andros boat was the talk of the marina. His sun-baked crew from Brunswick had caught their limit of huge mutton snapper, black grouper, and yellowtail snapper. The marina's photo board only held fifteen fish at a time. It took four separate hangings to get the entire catch photographed. Captain Rush had worked hard today. He caught live bait as the sun was rising and then fished the reef thirty miles southwest of Key West before trying out a new wreck he recently found by accident. While the northern tourists snacked, drank beer, and fried in the sun, Rush Maltz handled the anchor, chummed with live bait, and served lunch and drinks, all while teaching the family how to saltwater fish. It had been a very long day. And to top it off, while fishing at his new secret spot, an obnoxious-looking Jet Ski circled him twice. Although he could not read the colorful words on the side of the Sea-Doo, he was sure they were trying to steal his GPS coordinates. But then the man on the Jet Ski did something bizarre. He emptied some boxes of what looked like dry cement along with some plastic flowers that floated on the ocean's surface. Immediately a feeding frenzy of both birds and fish frothed the waters. And then the Jet Ski took off towards Key West disappearing quickly on the horizon. In all of Captain Rush's years, he had seen many unusual sights, but this one certainly ranked high on his list of peculiar. However, it would not be the most outlandish event he witnessed that day. On the way in, before returning to the Marina, Captain Rush rigged a spinning rod with a thirty-pound leader, no weight, and a live pilcher. He let the youngest son cast the bait into the frenzied waters near what looked like a plastic hibiscus. As a seagull was about to grab the bait from the surface, a huge mutton snapper attacked from below in an explosion that threw water on the diving bird. The young angler fought the thirty-pound snapper for twenty minutes before bringing him into the boat. He had caught the biggest snapper of the day, and his smile showed it.

After all of the photographs, unloading his charter's gear, food, and leftover beers, Rush started cleaning the catch. As he filleted each fish, the family recounted stories of their very fun and successful day. Murray, the marina's resident yellow-crowned night heron, stood tall on the cleaning table waiting for a tasty handout. A huge school of various sizes of tarpon filled the water below, charging any scrap of fish Rush discarded.

Rush saved the biggest mutton snapper until last to clean. For the little boy's sake, he made a big deal over the fish, and everyone on the dock came over to congratulate the young angler from Maine. As the large assembled crowd surrounded Captain Maltz, the boy's eyes were bulging with excitement as Rush cut into the fish. High fives were flying, the crowd was cheering, and the cameras were flashing. A attractive young lady in a very tiny bikini was videoing the entire event. She leaned over close with her iPhone, then jumped back and let out a sudden, piercing, bloodcurdling shriek while pointing at the fish. It startled the crowd, and all eyes were on the snapper's mouth. Rush picked up the filleted carcass by the tail to throw overboard to the feeding tarpon. And then it happened. As Rush tossed the backbone and head to the tarpon below something fell into the sink. The woman's second bellow could be heard in Miami. Everything went silent as Rush, along with the crowd, and the young boy from Maine stared at the severed human finger stuck to the bottom of the sink.

CHAPTER 21

As Limbo headed west around the popular island towards Garrison Bight Marina, the ride was calm and quiet. This early in the morning, he only saw a few runners as they jogged through Mallory Square towards Hog's Breath Saloon. A soft sea breeze brought with it a nice aromatic combination of sea salt, fishing smells from the shrimpers, and a hint of diesel fuel. Limbo took in a huge breath of air, loving every second.

When Limbo idled up to *Heads Up*, Charlie was waiting at the stern with a large cup of Con Leche in his left hand. Charlie arrived three hours earlier to clean, wash, and scrub up his boat before Limbo showed up. He made sure there were no fish scales, guts, blood, food, or trash left from his most recent trip to the Dry Tortugas with Hilda the Hun. It was a good thing Charlie was so thorough this morning. Some of the trash he found and discarded included a copy of *A Field Guide to the Birds of North America* and what looked like a brand new pair of Zeiss binoculars. One thing that was for sure, Hilda Tucker would never need them again.

Charlie helped Limbo aboard and stored his gear for the ride. With the calm seas and the huge outboards, Charlie figured he could run forty miles per hour. If his calculations were correct, they would arrive at Marina Hemingway in two and a half hours. It was a very comfortable ride, and Limbo complimented Charlie on his fine choice of boats. Even in the axis of the Gulf Stream with a three-foot chop, the *Heads Up* sliced through the waves like a knife through warm butter. They arrived in Cuba about ten o'clock in the morning. They would have been an hour earlier had they not stopped at a large weed line to troll for dolphin. The hour they fished was well worth the effort, as the four fish in the cooler were spectacular. The three bull dolphin and one cow all weighed over twenty-five pounds each.

Admiral Pap's directions once inside Marina Hemingway were skillfully accurate. Castillo was the name on the dark-skinned officer's uniform name tag who welcomed Charlie and Limbo to Cuba. With Limbo's command of the Cuban Spanish dialect along with the eight large dolphin fillets, Officer Castillo was polite and all smiles as he checked them in. Castillo was very methodical and precise with his inspection of the boat. Limbo sensed it was more about curiosity than security. The officer seemed intrigued over Charlie's boat.

"How fast will she go?" he asked in Spanish.

"La velocidad es de sesenta y cinco millas por hora," Limbo answered.

Next, the three men shared a Landshark beer from Charlie's ice chest.

Limbo and Officer Castillo sounded like old friends as they discussed Cuban-American relations, fishing, cigars, rum, music, and the life and death of Fidel. They thanked the officer, said goodbye and idled the boat through the small canal until they found the old cabin cruiser that matched the photo Admiral Pap had emailed to Limbo's phone.

The time was three o'clock, three hours before Dawn normally showed up. Charlie tied up the boat next to the cruiser, and he and Limbo walked through the marina.

"It looks more like a junkyard for old boats than a marina," Charlie said.

"Yeah, or a boat cemetery," Limbo answered.

Most of the boats were not seaworthy, and some were half sunk in the tannic colored water, trapped by the decaying seawalls that contain the canal. On land, large, intimidating billboards are a constant reminder of the revolution and victory for Fidel Castro and Che Guevara. Limbo had seen them before, but for Charlie, it was very disturbing.

Back at the boat, hoping Dawn would soon return Charlie said, "I heard Powell is in the clear now that Hilda disappeared off the face of the earth."

"I'm not sure about that, but no one seems to know what happened or where she is," Limbo replied.

Charlie smiled and said, "If you ask me, her vanishing is a blessing in disguise. She can't sue Powell now and ruin his business. Besides, she was a horrible person and certainly would have been arrested for extortion if she were still alive."

"Is she dead, Charlie?" Limbo asked.

"Well, I assumed she must be, but I guess we don't really know for certain," Charlie answered.

"I'm sure it's not over yet," Limbo said.

"No, it's like they say. It ain't over till the fat lady sings," Charlie said with maybe too much cheer in his voice.

Limbo looked up and was relieved to see Dawn walking their way. He was happy to change the conversation with Charlie and satisfied to see Dawn alive and well. She was a little thinner than he remembered but still as beautiful as ever. Her blonde hair was much longer and her clothes old and tattered.

Limbo always said that the older he got, he appreciated good memories as his greatest souvenirs. Seeing Dawn's face light up with her smile so big and her arms extended when she recognized Captain Limbo would be his most precious Cuban souvenir of all. The hug was as if a father had just found his only daughter after a lifetime apart. The emotion that flowed was so contagious, Charlie Switzer was crying like a baby with them. Limbo introduced Dawn and Charlie. A group hug with more tears followed.

Almost dark now, the *Heads Up* idled towards the marina's entrance. Dawn hid down below the console with the head, life jackets, and extra tackle. She was so excited and happy thinking of how it will be to hold Powell tight in her arms. She began to weep again.

Officer Castillo waved his new friends through with two thumbs up. Limbo returned the gesture and yelled, "Hasta luego, mi amigo."

Señor Castillo smiled big as Charlie pushed the throttle forward, jumping up on plane, heading back north to the southernmost tip of the good ole USA. The Gulf was flat calm with a slight south breeze and following seas. With such perfect weather conditions, Charlie pulled up to Garrison Bright Marina in ninety minutes.

Limbo called Powell as soon as he got back to his boat.

"Meet me at Hogfish Grill in thirty minutes, I have a surprise for you," Limbo hinted.

CHAPTER 22

Charlie Switzer sensed he needed to move swiftly. Sooner or later someone would notice Hilda the Horrible was missing.

"Not that anyone would actually care," Charlie thought to himself, but he knew he had to tie up loose ends and move quickly. Charlie was the kind of person who could acclimate and adapt to most situations, but prison was not one of them. By now, Charlie assumed Powell and Limbo both had questions and suspicions and may even have figured out what happened to Hilda, or at least who was to blame for her sudden disappearance.

Before resigning from the board of South Beach Bank, Charlie transferred three hundred twenty-six thousand dollars out of Hilda's account. Luckily Dr. James Adams and Charles Powell Taylor both had checking accounts at the bank. He smiled as he envisioned Limbo's and Powell's reaction when they realized Hilda Tucker had transferred one hundred sixty-three thousand dollars to each of them before she vanished. He was happy now for his new friends and better yet, the transfer could not be tracked back to him. People would assume Hilda was alive and well when the transaction occurred. But then again, Charlie did not yet know about the extraordinarily odd catch aboard Captain Rush Maltz's boat yesterday.

The gloomy forecast for tomorrow called for extremely bad weather to ravage the lower Keys. Sheltered from the storm, *Heads Up* was securely anchored in the privacy of the mangroves off Geiger Key. Charlie enjoyed both the protection and the solitude the hidden cove provided. It was here in this secluded hurricane hole that Charlie planned his escape and his future. He knew what had to be done, though he hated to leave Key West. Besides the fishing, new friends, the laid back Keys lifestyle, and the local hangouts, Charlie would miss being the King Conch of Fantasy Fest this year in October. It was an honor that is not easily acquired. However, Charlie had donated five hundred thousand dollars to benefit AIDS research on behalf of Fantasy Fest. This made him the most generous king since 1979 when the festival started. What a shame, Charlie thought as he stared into the clear shallow waters from the bow of his boat. Devin, his new friend at Caribbean Jewelers, had offered to paint his body, a custom associated with Fantasy Fest. Besides working for Powell, Devin was a world-class body painter. She had already purchased the crimson, gray, and white colors necessary to transform Charlie's naked torso into the University of Alabama's mascot, Big Al. It would have been a masterpiece and surely a hit on Duval Street.

Below a big block letter A painted in crimson would be a magnificent rendition of Al. His large elephant ears in gray painted on Charlie's stomach, and white tusks on each upper leg would extend from below a large gray trunk. A trunk that started at Charlie's belly button and ended at the head of his wrinkled penis. Charlie had planned on using several of the blue pills he received from Pfizer as a bonus to keep the trunk erect. Nothing could be worse than walking down Duval Street with a limp trunk, Charlie thought. Charlie laughed so loud with that thought it brought him back to the moment.

Sir Charlie's plan was a simple one, sell all of his shit, take plenty of cash with him, open a bank account for the rest in an alias name, and disappear in the Bahamas or maybe Cuba.

Charlie knew he only had a day or two before he would have to answer lingering questions. These questions, if answered incorrectly could put him behind bars for the remainder of his years. Charlie decided that tomorrow when the bad weather hit he would transfer the balances from his bank accounts into several different banks in the Bahamas and Cayman Islands. He had enough actual cash stashed for him to live easily for a year. By then, things will have settled down enough for him to retrieve whatever he needed. Next, it would be necessary to find a reliable realtor to sell his property on Duval Street along with his home. He would instruct Mr. Will Ozburn at N.A.I. Cayo Huesto Realty to wire the money to his stockbroker in Pensacola who would then forward it to one of his hidden Cayman accounts. By tomorrow evening, Charlie would donate any and all personal items, clothing, and tackle that would not fit on his boat to the Goodwill Store on Big Pine Key. His last stop would be the Caribbean Jewelry Company to say goodbye to Devin and give her the title to his Jet Ski. He would explain to her that he would be traveling overseas for the next few years and would be out of touch. It was a necessary lie.

Since Charlie had gotten cold feet about marriage and decided he did not want to commit to anyone, he still had the eight-carat diamond ring he purchased from Powell Taylor. He also knew now that he could not afford to have anyone know where he would be. A good attorney friend of his back in Pensacola once told him, "Charlie, there are three kinds of people in this world, friends, family, and witnesses." So, for now, having a fiancée with him was totally out of the question.

Charlie thought about giving the ring to Devin but changed his mind quickly. He could use it with much better results down island. In two days, three at the most, Charlie's SeaVee would be loaded with clothes, tackle, and cash. Captain Charles Switzer would begin his new adventure. Charlie Switzer's promise to himself before pursuing this new venture was simple. Heeding the sensible words of his attorney friend, Charlie would keep his cherished family and friends close and would leave no witnesses.

CHAPTER 23

The blistered tourists from Maine had just left Murray's Marina with their ice chests full of fillets and plenty of stories to retell when the Key West posse arrived. They came not on horses, but in fast cars with flashing lights and loud sirens. Monroe County was represented by its best. Officers from the Key West Police Department, marine patrol, the FBI, the sheriff's office, and the Coast Guard all came flying in from US 1 like fighter pilots on a target.

As soon as Captain Rush Maltz realized he had a severed human thumb fall out of a snapper's gullet when he was filleting him, he knew he had to call the authorities. Rush had contacted a friend of his at the marine patrol who sometimes chartered him for a fishing trip when he had family visiting. So he was quite surprised to see all of the different law enforcement vehicles swarm the parking lot with such a dramatic entrance. Rush's friend explained to him that since the thumb was originally in the ocean that Coast Guard had to be contacted. And since obviously, a severed body part suggests foul play he needed to also contact the FBI and local police along with the sheriff's department. Rush understood their reasoning but not all of the questioning that followed. He felt like he was being cross-examined as a suspect.

The marine patrol asked questions like, "Do you know the GPS coordinates where you caught the fish?"

The Coast Guard asked, "Were there any other boats there at the time?"

Rush pointed to the GPS map on the console of his boat to the exact location the fish was caught. Everyone made notes and wrote down the coordinates.

Rush then addressed the Coast Guard's question with careful attention to details. "I was fishing about two hundred yards away when I saw a Jet Ski dump something overboard at the location I caught the fish. The driver's behavior was a little erratic and bizarre I thought at the time."

"What do you mean erratic and bizarre?" an FBI agent asked.

"Well, once he dumped a few canisters of what looked like cement overboard, he then circled the area taking pictures. When all of the seagulls started feeding, and I saw fish slashing the surface, I assumed he had dumped chum overboard. I slowly headed his way to get a better look. I felt like I may have interrupted whatever he was doing because when he saw me coming, he took off at full speed heading north towards Key West."

"Was there anything else you noticed out of the ordinary? Anything strange or recognizable?" one of the uniformed officers asked.

Rush thought about it for a minute trying to re-create the scene in his mind. "Yes, yeah I do remember something strange. There were a couple of plastic flowers floating on the surface when I got there."

"What kind of flowers? What did they look like?" the FBI agent chimed in.

"I don't know, a flower, they were plastic and red, maybe pink I think," Rush answered with displeasure in his voice.

"Look, Captain Maltz, we are not trying to upset you, and we appreciate all of your help. Please think again. How about the Jet Ski? What color was it? Did it have numbers on the side? Is there anything you can tell us about the person driving?"

"I didn't get a good look at the Jet Ski. He took off in such a hurry I never got that close. But it was a man driving, and the Jet Ski had a bird painted on the side, maybe a couple. And it had a bunch of words that I could not make out written all over the sides," Rush replied.

"Were the birds blue and white?" a sheriff's deputy asked.

"Is that where you caught the grouper that had swallowed the finger?" the FBI agent added.

Rush acknowledged the deputy first, directed a stare his way and answered, "Yes, the birds were blue and white," wondering if that was just a good guess or not.

He then turned to address the FBI agent, "Yes, the water was alive with frenzied fish feeding, so I rigged the tackle for my clients. The young boy caught the fish with the severed thumb. By the way, it was a snapper, not a grouper that spit up the detached appendage," Rush said with a bit of sarcasm in his voice.

Rush placed the thumb in a baggie with some ice, held it up in the air and said, "Who wants it?"

After some discussion and much argument, they all concluded that the Key West Police Department had authority over the FBI. Besides, the officer with the KWPD said he thought he might have a good lead already. Rush's descriptions of the Jet Ski triggered something in the officer's memory.

A couple of weeks back the policeman's son was walking Duval Street with friends from out of town. They started at Truman Street heading north and planning to end up at Sloppy Joe's Bar. At the corner of Truman and Duval were attractive young tanned girls in bikinis handing out brochures to the tourists as they passed by. The boys, of course, stopped to check them out in hopes of hooking up later at Sloppy Joes. They eagerly listened to the girls' sales pitches and gathered brochures for all kinds of water activities and tours. However, the officer's son noticed one unusual pamphlet amidst all of the sailboat rides, fishing, snorkel and dive trips, sunset cruises, parasailing, and Tortugas tours. It was the only brochure he brought home to show his parents.

All of the original posse had left Murray's Marina except the officer from the Key West Police Department.

"Hey Captain Rush, you mind coming out to my patrol car for a minute? I have something I want to show you."

Rush was happy to help. Had it been the FBI agent it might have been a different story. Rush felt the agent had a bad attitude. The officer and Rush sat in the hot patrol car while the policeman rifled through papers in the glove compartment.

"My son brought me a brochure from Duval Street. It's in here somewhere I know. We all had a laugh about it over dinner that night, but I'll be damned if it may be a huge clue," the officer said.

He finally found what he was looking for and with much relief opened the brochure pointing to the first page and said, "There, look. Is that the Jet Ski, Captain?"

"Holy shit! That's it! For sure, Officer, that is it!" Rush exclaimed.

The Southernmost Sea Burial brochure was opened to the page that explained the Sea Gull Package. Pointing to the flowers in the picture Rush said, "This is exactly what I saw, Officer, right down to the pink flowers."

"They're hibiscus," the officer said.

"Okay," Rush said with no enthusiasm.

"You think he dumped the thumb overboard with the owner's ashes?" Rush continued.

Looking at the back page of the brochure the officer answered, "I'm not sure, Captain Maltz, but that will be the first question I ask Mr. Charles Switzer when I see him."

CHAPTER 24

When I arrived at Hogfish Grill, the sun had long set over Stock Island. I could not imagine what was on Limbo's mind this evening. When he called, he sounded so upbeat and excited about something. On the ride over, I racked my brain for a reason. Could it have something to do with Hilda? Or maybe Charlie Switzer? Maybe they both left town and ran away together forever. Now that would be interesting and highly unlikely. But knowing Limbo, it could be something as simple as he just found out that it's ladies night at Louie's Backyard.

With a serpentine slither, I made my way through the maze of picnic tables on the outer deck. Even with the dark sky, I was able to spot Limbo's faded car parked near the water under a coconut palm. A few tourists gathered under each of the lights that were mounted on posts over the water. They seemed mesmerized by something in the water. They watched in awe, never glancing away, as tarpon rolled below. I would have joined them to observe the choreographed underwater fish dance in the spotlight, but I needed to find Limbo. I wasn't sure what was so important, but I also had some very interesting news for him tonight. On the way out the door, I grabbed my mail to read. I opened my bank statement as I always do, just to check my ending balance. Expecting to see less than five hundred dollars in the account, I was taken aback with the figure I saw. I studied the statement closer and noticed that a few days ago someone deposited one hundred and sixty-three thousand dollars into my account.

"Hey Powell, over here!" Limbo yelled from across the bar.

When my eyes caught up with his voice, I noticed he was in tan linen slacks, an ironed black shirt with palm trees and real shoes. What the hell? I thought. Limbo never wears shoes. I didn't even know he owned a pair. He is always barefooted unless shoes are required which forces him into flip flops. He must have a girlfriend, I thought.

When I sat down across the picnic table from him, Limbo looked as nervous as a whore in the communion line.

"What's up, Limbo? You okay?" I asked.

"Yeah, yes! I'm better than okay. I'm ecstatic in fact. I've never felt so good in my entire life. I am on cloud nine, could not be any better. It's the best day of my life, my friend."

"Whoa! Stop!" I shouted, "What the hell is it?"

"Well, sit down, and I'll tell you," he said.

"I am sitting," I replied.

"Oh yeah, I see. Okay, well where do I start? You remember the last time we met at Geiger Key Marina?"

"Yes, Limbo, I remember. I came in my skiff after fishing Sugarloaf, and you came in your favorite car," I said.

"Do you remember what we talked about?" he asked.

I had to think for a minute, trying to retrieve conversation from my memory. Thinking out loud I whispered, "Fishing, Woodie, Beers. Oh wait, I remember we talked about Cuba and Dawn."

"Yes, Dawn, that's it."

"That's it? What about it? What about Dawn?" I asked anxiously.

"I was right, Powell, she's alive! I knew it, she is alive and well!" Limbo was twitching and shaking as if he were strapped to an electric chair.

"What?" I hardly could whisper. "Are you sure?"

"No question," Limbo exclaimed as he pointed behind me.

When I stood up and turned, there she was standing only a few feet away. I could not even process what my eyes were seeing. Dawn Landry, more beautiful than I remembered with her glistening blonde hair, ravishing smile, and vivid hypnotic blue eyes ran towards me with open arms. The unrecognizable primal, guttural bellow that escaped from my lips sounded more like a gator in heat than the joyous tone I was hoping for. I simply could not believe what I was seeing.

Over the past eight months, I had mournfully and painfully accepted Dawn's senseless, brutal death. I was certain she had died that night in the explosion aboard the ship in Havana. And now here I was reaching out to hold her tight and vowed that I would never again let her go. With tears flowing down both of our cheeks I wished this feeling would last forever.

"I love you so much, Powell," Dawn said through sobs.

I pushed back so I could see into her eyes and said, "Dawn, I'm so sorry. I will never let anything bad happen to you again. I love you."

When we finally were able to separate, I grabbed Dawn's hand and turned towards Limbo. Not only was he crying like a baby, but half of the restaurant was doing the same. And then, from behind the bar, Bobby the owner announced, "Powell, dinner is on me. Go get a room."

The entire restaurant broke into much-needed laughter that drowned out the applause.

In the parking lot, Dawn hugged Limbo and said, "Thank Charles for me too, please."

I looked at Limbo as he stared back my way with one eyebrow lifted and said, "She'll explain."

He jumped in Woodie and disappeared down the road honking the horn and waving out the window like a kid in a parade.

On the trip back to Cudjoe Key, Dawn explained how Limbo and someone named Charlie Switzer dramatically and heroically rescued her by boat.

"They were so nice and sweet. I love Limbo, and Charlie was so kind to me. They are both such great people to have taken such a risk to help me."

I just smiled and said, "Yeah Dawn, I love Limbo too. He is a dear friend." I did not mention Charlie. I was pretty sure he was behind Hilda's disappearance and suspected he was responsible for the hundred and sixty-three thousand dollars that mysteriously showed up on my bank register. That reminded me that I needed to talk with Limbo about that deposit. But it would have to wait. I had other plans for this evening.

When we arrived back at my house, Dawn was thrilled to be back in a familiar place, a place she had feared she would never see again. As exhausted as she was, Dawn wanted to talk and hold each other tight. We showered and slipped naked beneath the linen sheets. Holding each other close, we talked for about a minute and a half. She smelled of fresh soap, our bodies were still damp from the shower as I pulled her close. She pressed her lips to mine. It was as if we were making love for the first time ever. Heat lightning over Cudjoe Bay constantly crept through the bedroom window. Dawn jumped, but I pulled her back close. After being apart for so long, our sensual encounter was emotional. I felt trust, respect, companionship, friendship, pleasure, and happiness. But also I sensed a little guilt. When I felt Dawn's body quiver and then heard her quietly weeping, I realized it was even more complicated for her. I kissed her forehead and told her how happy I was to have her back in my life.

"I love you," she whispered as she fell asleep in my arms.

CHAPTER 25

Captain Limbo was relaxing in chill mode after smoking a little "train wreck" when the sound of the phone ringing scared the shit out of him. He had smoked the entire joint and drunk a six-pack, which explained why he tripped jumping towards the telephone trying to answer it.

"Yeah, hello, uh, Limbo Adams here," he mumbled.

"Did I wake you up or something?" Powell asked.

"Uh-huh, I think so."

"Well, sober up and get over here right away. You won't believe what I got in the mail today. Hurry up! Dawn and I are waiting on you," Powell continued.

Limbo decided to brew some strong coffee and take a short swim before heading east on US 1 to see Powell. He had always heard that loose lips sink ships and he figured if those lips were swimming in an ocean of alcohol in the wake of smoking a fat one, a massive shipwreck was inevitable. Limbo's brain protected too many deep dark secrets from his past. He was not about to let down his guard allowing any of his obscure, hidden, suppressed stories to escape now.

When Limbo and Woodie finally arrived at Powell's, the hands on his dive watch said six forty-five. Before he could open the car door, Powell and Dawn met him outside.

Dawn, laughing uncontrollably, said, "Wow Limbo, Powell was right. Now that I see it in the daylight, you do have an awesome Woodie. But it's a lot smaller than I had pictured."

Limbo smiled and felt glad about Dawn and Powell being back

together. He never got tired of the jokes about his all-time favorite station wagon with the faded, peeling wooden sides.

"Come on inside, Limbo. Join us for dinner before I share with you the big bombshell revelation," Powell said.

Limbo was curious. He was also very hungry, and his mind was finally beginning to clear again, so he did not argue. He followed the loving reconnected couple to the outside deck where a delicious-looking meal on a beautifully set table awaited. It was natural to see Powell and Dawn so incredibly happy again. They seemed to have taken up right where they left off and were making up for lost time. Holding hands, sneaking a kiss, laughing and joking, Powell and Dawn were obviously still madly in love. Dawn had much to celebrate this night. She was very fortunate and overjoyed to be back home, thankful for another chance at life and tickled to death about her future with Powell.

In celebration, Dawn had prepared a lower Keys feast tonight with an added Cuban flair. She sautéed some fresh cut chunks of lobster in a skillet with some garlic, red pepper flakes, butter, parsley, basil, and goat cheese. She served it over saffron rice with some black beans on the side. She saved her favorite key lime pie recipe for later. Also in celebration, Powell opened a bottle of 2013 Caymus Special Selection Cabernet. Although Dawn and Powell were very anxious to show Limbo their discovery, dinner seemed to last forever. The three friends took turns toasting everything from luck, love, and life, to the ocean, the Keys, and just how aromatic the smell of monkey shit in the air was tonight.

It was finally time for dessert and the finale for the evening. Dawn cut everyone a generous slice of key lime pie and refilled the wine glasses. Powell announced, "Sit back and enjoy the movie, it's show time."

The DVD was addressed to Powell Taylor, Jr. with a note that simply said, "It's Over."

Sipping the last of many bottles of the red wine and eating the best key lime pie Limbo had ever tasted, three sets of eyeballs bulged out as laughter, along with revulsion, filled the back deck.

In high definition filling the entire television screen was a disgusting, nude, obviously drunk fat lady singing a tune from the *Sound of*

Music.

"So long, farewell, auf weidersehen, goodnight. I hate to go and leave this pretty sight."

The smiles disappeared as quickly as her picture on the screen.

"How did he get Hilda to do that?" Powell whispered.

Limbo raised his glass and replied, "Who cares, Powell. Charlie's gone out of our lives, and the fat lady has sung."

CHAPTER 26

I woke up early, a little after sunrise and quietly threw on some shorts and a t-shirt. I gently closed the door behind me so Dawn could get some well-deserved rest. I took my coffee out on the back deck, sat down, and reminisced about all the good times Dawn and I had shared together. It felt great to have her back home.

I decided I needed to call Limbo this morning before Dawn woke up. We needed to discuss the large amount of money that showed up in my checking account. I was sure that as exhausted as Dawn must have been, she would sleep until noon. I fixed myself another cup of coffee, grabbed my cell phone, and sat down on the back deck. There was a slight south wind today bringing with it all the familiar smells from Monkey Island. I knew I was wasting my time as I dialed Charlie Switzer's cell phone. I heard the same message as when I called his work and home phones. "Sorry, you have reached a number that has been disconnected at the owner's request."

I figured Charlie was long gone after seeing the horrific video of Hilda's song. I was also certain that Charlie Switzer had murdered Hilda Tucker that night on his boat.

I was about to dial Limbo when I heard someone drive up out front. I jumped up and opened the front door before a knock or doorbell could awaken Dawn. In the driveway sat a sad Woodie with its faded paint, peeling shellac, and bald tires. If it were in mint condition, it would truly be a collector's item worth plenty. But for Limbo, the interesting history and the fact that it was a conversation piece wherever he went made it all the more valuable to him. As Limbo told everyone, his Woodie was old but dependable.

As I was looking around searching for Limbo, I heard my phone ringing and someone beating on the back door. In fact, it sounded more like someone trying to break in. I grabbed my phone and answered it on the run.

"Powell, it's Devin. I need to talk to you. It's important."

"Hang on a minute, Devin. Someone's beating on my door."

I let Limbo in the back as Dawn entered the kitchen in her robe and slippers with a bad case of bed head. When she saw Limbo, she ran back into the bedroom embarrassed, "Sorry, I didn't know we had company."

"Hey Devin, can I call you right back in five minutes?" I asked.

"Yes, but hurry up. Like I said, it's fucking important," she fired back.

I sat Limbo down on the back deck after he helped himself to some coffee.

"I'll be right back," I told him.

I fixed Dawn a cup of coffee and took it back as a peace offering. "I didn't realize Limbo was coming over this morning, or that the phone would ring so early."

"I was ready to get up anyway. I just love being back here. Besides, I'm so pale, I want to lay out and get some sun," Dawn answered.

She looked so beautiful standing there in the new black bikini I was tempted to run Limbo off. But I didn't because we had to have the conversation about Charlie that was long overdue.

When I sat down with Limbo, I explained that I needed to call Devin back and how important she said it was.

"Okay, but I have something important to discuss too," Limbo said.

Of course, I had already concluded that since he was here an hour after sunrise beating on my back door. I dialed Devin's number, and she answered on the first ring.

"It took you long enough! What the fuck?" she said.

"What's so important? And can you please try not to talk like a drunken sailor when you tell me?" I asked.

As she told me her story, I was amazed and intrigued but not surprised in the least. Limbo listened quietly, gathering what info he could, trying to process what he was overhearing and make sense of it all.

"Charlie came by the store a couple days ago and gave me his Jet Ski. He said he was going to travel the world for a couple years. At the time, I thought it was so nice of him, but he seemed to be in such a huge hurry," Devin told me.

I didn't tell her about the video and that I already assumed he left town. I just tried to listen as my mind searched for any hints as to where Charlie could have gone.

Then Devin continued, "Have you seen the paper this morning?"

"No, I haven't had time to read the paper," I answered.

Limbo picked up on that and ran and retrieved the newspaper off of my front steps. As I listened to Devin, I could not help watching Limbo's facial expressions as he read.

"Well, yesterday some cop came by here asking me all about Charlie Switzer and why he gave me a Jet Ski. Somehow he traced the title from a picture in Charlie's sea burial brochure. He took the picture to the tag office in Key West. They were able to identify Charlie as the owner from the numbers on the hull. And of course, the title showed me as the new owner."

"What did you tell him?" I asked.

"Nothing, not a fucking thing. I mean not a thing," she answered.

Devin then told me how the police officer suspected her of being involved with Charlie and thought she may know where he was. She explained that she was gay and had a longtime girlfriend and that Charlie was just an acquaintance who shopped in the store.

After an hour, when the officer finally left, Devin was sure she had convinced him she had no knowledge as to the whereabouts of one Charles Switzer.

"Go read the paper, Powell. It explains a lot. No wonder Charlie left the country," she said as she hung up.

As I laid down the phone, I noticed Dawn out by the canal, lying face down on a lounge chair with only her bikini bottoms on. How great it was to have a second chance.

I looked over at Limbo and raised one eyebrow. He held up the paper and said to me, "Holy mother of god, you won't believe this. But at least it explains the money."

SEVERED HUMAN THUMB FOUND IN MUTTON SNAP-PER IDENTIFIED

After reading the article on the front page of the *Key West Times*, Limbo and I both concluded that it was surely Charlie Switzer who put the one hundred sixty-three thousand dollars into each of our bank accounts. He had obviously lied earlier when he told us that Hilda had transferred all of her money to an offshore account in Panama. We reluctantly came to accept his dishonesty and assumed it was just to buy some time. We knew that Charlie had deposited Hilda's money into our accounts. And we were also convinced that Charlie Switzer did indeed murder Hilda Tucker. He had to have used her thumb to open her account and transfer the balance to Limbo and me. I could not help but think as dishonest and gross as Hilda the Hun was, why Charlie felt the need to kill her. Was it to help me out, to keep her from filing the lawsuit? Did he do it to impress Devin? Was it just because she was loathsome and a burden on society? Was it just a sport killing out of boredom by someone who seemed to have it all, or could it be something more?

I glanced down at Dawn. She had turned over and placed the top of her swimsuit across her breasts.

CHAPTER 27

The KWPD detective who was investigating the disappearance of Hilda Tucker and Charlie Switzer was Sergeant Luis Ramirez. He was of Cuban descent and had worked long and hard and had put in many hours to become a sergeant. Luis was very methodical and thorough in every investigation, but especially with this one. He was a bit intrigued with the strange circumstances that had turned up the key evidence. "What are the chances of finding a human thumb that had been tossed overboard miles offshore," he thought.

Sergeant Ramirez had tracked the Jet Ski to Devin Drake at Caribbean Jewelers with a title from the previous owner. On Mr. Charles Switzer's paperwork, he had listed the Key West Branch of South Beach Bank and Trust as his financial institution. Sergeant Ramirez had identified the human thumb from fingerprints on file as belonging to a Hilda Tucker. With Hilda's shady past and multiple arrests, the fingerprint match was actually much easier than he had anticipated. The sergeant was pretty sure that Charlie Switzer was responsible for the disappearance of Hilda Tucker. It was a gut feeling and all of the evidence so far pointed him in that direction. While trying to find a motive or connection between the two, he discovered that Charlie not only had an account at South Beach Bank and Trust, he was also a board member. While looking closer into Hilda's background, he exposed her nasty occupation of slip-and-fall lawsuits resulting in thousands of dollars paid by her targets. Thousands of dollars that she deposited into the same bank branch where Mr. Charles Switzer served on their board. This information opened up an entire new bucket of worms.

"Things are getting very interesting in this case," he had shared with his wife at dinner last night. But even after twenty-two years of marriage, he never discussed details from any investigation. This case would be no different. He felt it could possibly put his family in danger and would most probably jinx his mojo.

On his second day visiting the bank, the president of the branch was eager to help Luis get all of the answers he needed. He showed the sergeant all of the newest in banking technology which included the latest in optical fingerprint scanners. This was, naturally, of great interest to Sergeant Ramirez.

"Would you mind showing me all of the banking activity for the past month on both Mr. Switzer's accounts and Ms. Turner's?" the sergeant asked.

The bank president sat Luis down at a computer and pulled up the accounts. As he scrolled down, he made notes, checked them, and rechecked them.

"Wow, that is very odd," the sergeant said.

"What?" the banker asked.

"Well, Ms. Turner disappeared over a week and a half ago. I know because her power was cut off, her house was cleaned out, and her mail stopped then. When did you say Mr. Switzer resigned from your bank board?" Ramirez said.

"About the same time. Oh, I see. That is odd," the banker replied.

"Yes it is, but not as odd as this," the detective said pointing at Hilda's bank statement.

When the bank president looked more closely, he noticed that Hilda had transferred all of her money out of her account two days after she disappeared.

"How do you explain that, sir? How can someone transfer all of their money without being present?" Ramirez asked.

"It's impossible detective. There's no way. Ms. Tucker had to come in that day herself. She had to be present. Unless of course someone cut off her right thumb and fooled the scanner," the banker said with loud laughter.

"You don't read the paper do you, sir?" Sergeant Ramirez sarcastically asked.

The banker's puzzled look on his face answered the question as Sergeant Luis Ramirez shook his limp hand, said goodbye, and walked out of the bank.

When the detective returned to his desk back at the station, he glanced over his notes before running off to his appointment on Duval Street. Looking at his notes, the only loose ends from the bank were two people that he assumed Charlie Switzer gave Hilda's money to. He would contact Mr. Powell Taylor, Jr. and Dr. James Adams tomorrow.

When Ramirez arrived at the closed building that was home to Southernmost Sea Burial, Will Ozburn greeted him with the key. The detective had jotted down the name of his realty company off of the sign in the front window yesterday. When Mr. Ozburn realized that Sergeant Ramirez was not a prospective buyer, he lost interest quickly.

"Look, Officer, I really have better things to do than give you a tour of the Duval Dungeon here. No offense, but this place creeps me out, and if you're not interested in purchasing, I have other things to do," the arrogant realtor complained.

"Well, Will, I don't really give a rat's ass what you think or what you would rather be doing. You're gonna show me around and answer my questions. And you're gonna do it with a smile on your face, or perhaps you would prefer to go back to the station and answer my questions there?" Ramirez barked back.

With an adjusted attitude, Mr. Ozburn gladly showed the detective around and answered all of his questions to the best of his knowledge.

"So, you are sure you have never met Charles Switzer or have never laid eyes on him?"

"Yes sir, I'm positive," Ozburn replied.

The nervous realtor then told the sergeant that he did not know where Charlie was, had not heard from him in a week and had no contact information at all on him.

"How are you supposed to get in touch with him if you sell his building and house?" Ramirez asked.

Will Ozburn explained that Charlie Switzer said he would call once a month to check in. When his property sold, he was to wire the money to his stockbroker's account. He would give those instructions when the time came. It was somewhere in Pensacola or maybe in the islands, but just where the realtor could not remember. If not Pensacola, it could possibly be the Bahamas or the Caymans maybe. The hostility between the detective and the realtor made it much easier for Will Ozburn to tell the lie. Ramirez told Ozburn that he expected a call as soon as he heard from Charlie Switzer.

"Yes sir, will do Sergeant," the realtor told him. Of course, that was just another lie, which obviously came easily for Will Ozburn.

Driving back to his realty office, Will smiled greedily thinking about his big payday when he sells Charlie Switzer's property. Charlie called him yesterday from the Oceanfront Grand Floridian Hotel in Islamorada to check in. The plan they agreed on would be profitable for both. Will was to wait until both properties sold keeping the money in his account at The Bank of America on Flagler Avenue in Key West. Will knew the properties were both exclusive and in high demand. The sale of his home and the building on Duval Street would easily bring six and a half million dollars. When the deal was completed, Charlie would call Will from a disposable cell phone with instructions to wire the money to his offshore Cayman account, not to his Pensacola stockbroker. It's an account Charlie already had set up using an alias. When the money was securely deposited, Charlie planned to immediately transfer the funds to a Bahamian bank set up in another alias. Once that was done, Charlie would call Will and tell him it is okay to contact the authorities and give them the name of the bank in the Cayman Islands. For this favor, Will Ozburn's commission on the sale will be one point five million dollars. The thought of double-crossing Charlie never entered Will Ozburn's mind. He would be more than well compensated, and besides, he didn't want to be found floating tits up in the ocean with digits missing. Unlike the president of South Beach Bank and Trust, Will Ozburn did read the paper.

CHAPTER 28

As soon as the weather cleared, Charlie pulled out of the Mangroves behind Geiger Key and ran up to Islamorada to tie up some loose ends. From his cell phone sitting oceanside at the Grand Floridian Hotel, he studied his plan as he always did. He read and reread his notes, rationally thought out every scenario, eliminated any unforeseen problems, and lastly, executed his plan.

"Damn, I miss this so much," he thought to himself.

This would be the most important marketing plan of his life. It had to be successful. There was no room for error. Although Charlie was often cocky and too sure of himself, he could not afford to be wrong this time. Charlie was surprised how easy it was to open offshore accounts on Grand Cayman and in the Bahamas all over the phone and with e-mail. He also felt good after the conversation with his Key West realtor, Will Ozburn. He knew the realtor was just shady enough and greedy enough to be unethical. Charlie's managerial abilities included how to read people, and he was right on the mark with Mr. Ozburn.

The next step in Charlie's well-designed plot would take him back across the Gulf Stream. He was hoping his new friend, Officer Castillo, at Marina Hemingway would be glad to see him. To ensure he would be, Charlie would arrive bearing gifts.

When Charlie departed the dock the next morning from Islamorada, the *Heads Up* was loaded with all of his worldly possessions. If he had forgotten anything, he would just buy it when he finally settled in the Bahamas. Besides his clothing, fishing tackle, important papers, and a pile of hidden cash, Charlie brought with him a case of Yuengling and a bottle of Pappy Van Winkle 20 Year Bourbon Whiskey. He wanted to make sure Officer Castillo would be happy to see him.

To the best of his knowledge, Charlie did not think anyone would be actively looking for him yet. Although he was fairly sure Powell, Limbo, and Devin suspected what he might have done, he was confident they would keep quiet. With those thoughts in his mind, he was in no hurry to race to Havana. When he passed a big weed line about forty miles offshore, he decided to fish it. Trolling three lines, two way back and one short, with green and yellow lures, the first dolphin hit within ten minutes. It was a nice cow about twenty pounds. In another five minutes, both reels screamed out. Behind the boat, two very large bull dolphins jumped and ran in opposite directions. Charlie left the boat in gear slowly moving forward as he reeled the first fish in while trying to keep an eye on the other reel. He was able to gaff the dolphin, throw him in the ice chest and grab the other line without losing either fish. The two fish weighed over forty pounds each, the biggest Charlie had every boated. As he closed the lid on the ice chest after placing the second fish on ice, something in the water caught his eye. About fifty chicken dolphins had followed the bulls up and were circling the boat in a spectacular frenzy. The water lit up with neon colors of blues and greens reflecting from the sides of the juvenile dolphin. Charlie grabbed a fly rod he had rigged with a small chartreuse and white fly and began casting. On every cast, an explosion erupted as ten fish tried to devour the fly as soon as it floated to the surface. Charlie caught and released about fifteen of the small acrobats before deciding it was time to turn back south. He washed down the deck, stowed the fly rod and tackle, and continued his leisurely path towards Havana.

"What a perfect day," Charlie thought to himself. He wished his new friends, Powell and Limbo could have been with him this day. And then he began to think what a shame that he would never see them or any of his friends or family again. As upsetting as that thought was to Charlie, he had always known this was a very strong possibility and an unfortunate hazard of the job. The money was good, and he would have it no other way. Besides, it was too late now for Charlie Switzer to ever turn back. His need for greed left too many skeletons in his closet and bodies in his wake. The thought saddened him as he readjusted the GPS track towards Marina Hemingway. Charlie switched on the autopilot sat back relaxing as he mentally rehearsed his plan of escape. Had he known what all was going on back in Key West, who was alerted and involved, he would have been in a much bigger hurry to get to Havana.

When *Heads Up* idled into the canal of Marina Hemingway, Charlie could see the huge smile as Officer Castillo waved him in.

"Hola, Señor Charles," he yelled.

Charlie returned the gesture, unloaded the beer and rare whiskey, and hopped up onto the dock. Although the gifts were not necessary, Officer Castillo came close to tears as he hugged his new friend, the expatriate American. The two drank a cold beer together while talking about Charlie's travels. But of course, very little that Charlie told Castillo was truthful.

Charlie found a little room to rent in old town Havana. He wanted to hit a few bars and get some photos of places he had heard of, but first, he needed to find an attractive young Cuban girl to share his forty-eight-hour experience. He would visit a cigar factory, La Bodequita del Medio, Hemmingway's house, and La Floridita during the days and The Tropicana Club at night. And then he would party and have sex all night with his *señorita bonita*. He could only allow himself a short time in Cuba. Charlie Switzer did not plan on being a fugitive for long. After spending two days in "Havana Town" taking in the sights, sipping mojitos and daiquiris while luring the señoritas to bed, Sir Charles set sail for a short stop in Miami aboard *Heads Up* around midnight in hopes to disappear forever. He would surely miss the life he had created and especially the lifestyle that came with it, but then again, the island life would not be bad either, he thought.

In an effort to cover his tracks, Charlie knew he could leave no obvious trails. He had to be smart and pay attention to every detail. Once he received word from his realtor, Mr. Ozburn, that the sale of his property was final, Charlie had to move quickly. After verifying that the funds had been deposited into his Cayman account, Charlie decided to fly to Grand Cayman and personally introduce himself. He hoped his new identity would serve him well and never be discovered. With the connections he had back in Miami, he was able to get all of the necessary documents that would keep him hidden from all persons that may want to find Mr. Charles Switzer. His new passport, driver's license, birth certificate, Bahamian bank accounts, and his house in the Bahamas were all listed under his new name, Mr. Alton Curtis Pinder.

The same acquaintances in Miami from his questionable past were also able to help Charlie Switzer dispose of his boat, *Heads Up*. They made it possible for Alton Pinder to purchase a newer slightly larger version of Charlie's old boat. Alton's new fifty-three-foot Hydra-Sport center console which he arrogantly named, *Thumbs Up* carried four Yamaha three hundred fifty horsepower outboards on the stern. The trip from Miami to his secretive island home had only taken three and a half hours. This gave Alton the needed time to revisit his strategy for Charlie Switzer's disappearance. "Safety is in the details," Charlie had always believed and even more so now. One of his most clever details occurred by accident and a lot of luck.

When Charlie had first purchased his boat, *Heads Up,* he had intended to use it mainly for shark fishing. There was something mystifying to him about a fish that had lived in the ocean over four hundred million years and had evolved into our modern day shark. Charlie also liked the empty dead stare in a shark's black eye. He enjoyed watching the television programs during Shark Week that featured massive shark attacks. The rage, the blood, the gnashing of teeth gave Charlie Switzer so much pleasure. When Charlie prepared a body for burial at sea before the cremation, he would always extract enough blood to fill a one-quart mason jar. He had read that a shark could smell one drop of blood in one million pints of sea water. When Charlie left Key West unexpectedly, the refrigerator in his funeral home held thirty-four jars of human blood. And although he never got the chance to chum up sharks with the blood, he packed two of the jars for his departure. The two quarts of blood he gave to his friends in Miami were both O-negative, the same blood type that ran through his own veins.

CHAPTER 29

When we received the phone calls from Detective Luis Ramirez neither Limbo nor I were surprised. It was only a matter of time as we had been expecting someone to contact us before now. From the information we read in the newspaper article, we realized it would not take long to link us to Charlie Switzer, Hilda, and the missing three hundred and twenty-six thousand dollars. The two of us spent yesterday afternoon and most of last night discussing what and how we would answer Sergeant Ramirez's questions.

Limbo and I were torn on just how to handle it. First, we tried to understand Charlie's motives and then discussed if we should turn on him and throw him under the bus. It was a difficult decision. Charlie, no doubt, had a huge and likable personality. His outgoing, friendly almost obnoxious persona was not only welcoming, but it was also quite refreshing. Although we both had reservations about him since the day we met him, he was always kind, helpful, and genuinely wanted to be our friend.

"He did not hesitate to agree immediately when I asked him to take me to Cuba in his boat to look for Dawn," Limbo said.

And I thought of how considerate I felt he was being when he was so concerned about Hilda filing a lawsuit against me. But that brought us back to the question that keeps nagging us. Why did Charlie feel it necessary to kill Hilda Tucker? After a few sleepless nights and much thought, I decided he did it out of friendship for me. I convinced myself that he wanted to protect me and prove his friendship. Why else would he deposit a hundred and thirty some thousand dollars in my account risking being caught?

Limbo had other reasoning for Charlie's need to murder Hilda the Hun, if, in fact, he did. After seeing her sing "Farewell" on the horrid video Charlie sent us, there wasn't much doubt.

"I think it was because of Charlie's self-absorbed, self-centered need for attention personality," Limbo exclaimed. Captain Limbo had always had a feeling that Charlie could be a bit abusive.

"I've never met an abusive person that was not self-centered," he said. "Although all abusive people are self-absorbed, not all self-centered people are abusive."

Limbo believed that personalities like Charlie's saw the world through a very different lens than the rest of us. Friendships or people that would be useful to Charlie were given more importance.

"Like the friendships he invented with you and me, Powell," Limbo said.

"How could I be useful to Charlie?" I asked.

"For some reason, he needed your friendship, he wanted badly to be your friend," Limbo replied.

Limbo also thought that people or other matters that didn't directly relate to Charlie were useless to him. He gave them little attention if any at all.

"I'm sure he has a narcissistic personality disorder, an exaggerated self-importance and a lack of empathy for those that disgust him. And that is where Hilda the Hun fits in," Limbo presented.

"Wow! You have put some thought into this, haven't you?" I said.

"Not really. I just knew someone once that was so depressed with her life she became very self-absorbed. Her behavior reminds of Charlie," Limbo said sadly.

But even with Dr. Limbo's diagnosis, we both still strangely liked Charlie Switzer. Maybe he had a disorder, maybe he was sick, but he always treated the two of us like his friends. Unfortunately, Hilda could not say the same thing. The bottom line that kept haunting us in our conversations was simply put when Limbo said, "Charlie Switzer is a murderer."

When we met Sergeant Ramirez at his office this morning, Limbo and I had not made any decisions. We just decided to listen to the questions and see where it took us. I did, however, bring the video of Hilda's last moments alive that Charlie had filmed. But I wasn't sure if I would hand it over or not.

"Please call me Luis," the detective said as we made our introductions. "Can I get you something to drink? Would you like some coffee, water, or a soft drink?" he asked.

We both declined his obvious overkill hospitality.

Sergeant Ramirez, I mean Luis, was very friendly and quite good at interrogation. It did not take him long to get to the point. He started by asking us about our relationships with Charlie Switzer and Hilda Tucker and how we had met. I told him about Charlie buying a huge diamond from me and that he had opened his business next door to mine on Duval Street. I explained that I knew Charlie first and that Limbo had only met him through me. After that, he directed most of his questions in my direction.

"So you and Charlie were good friends?" he asked.

"No, not at all. We were merely acquaintances through business," I answered.

Luis looked me in the eye and after a very dramatic ten-second pause said, "Acquaintances? Okay, if you say so. How about Hilda Tucker? What was that relationship?" a more serious Ramirez asked.

I explained the entire saga, a very descriptive version leaving no details out. I wanted him to know I was cooperative and trying to help him in any way I could. Well, that is not exactly accurate. I did it because I was sure he already knew the truth and the entire circumstance surrounding Hilda's disappearance. I didn't want him to sense I was hiding any facts or dark secrets.

"Okay, Mr. Taylor—"

"Please call me Powell," I interrupted.

"Like I was about to say, Mr. Taylor, if you were just acquaintances with Charlie Switzer and your friend here really didn't know him, how do you explain the three of you fishing the Tortugas together aboard his boat? And why would Dr. Adams here travel to Havana, Cuba, with a stranger?

And just how many times did you all get together socially? For instance let's say, dining at Santiago's Bodega. If you were involved with attorneys and lawsuits with Hilda Tucker, why in the hell would she give you two all of the money she had to her name?"

Well, I must say I was taken aback. I tried not to show my surprise or act like I was caught off-guard. I was concerned when I realized that Detective Ramirez had thoroughly looked into our backgrounds. He knew that Limbo was James Adams and had a doctorate degree. When I began to address his concerns, I only hoped he did not know our entire past history together.

During the next forty-five minutes, I felt I was able to successfully convince Luis Ramirez that Charlie Switzer was neither friends with Limbo or with me. I explained the fishing trip as an early business outing that I agreed upon while trying to sell him an expensive, large, flawless diamond ring. I took Limbo along as my friend who loves to fish. It was that simple. We had all gone to dinner in that same period of time for the same reasons. I sold him an eight-carat diamond engagement ring for over eight hundred and ninety-nine thousand dollars, and that was the last time I saw him. That was the end of it. I acted a little annoyed for having to explain to him when I told him I was not to blame for Hilda's disappearance or anything Mr. Switzer might have done.

"And I don't appreciate you treating me like a suspect, Luis!" I said with extra emphasis on his name.

Picking up on my frustration, Limbo masterfully told a tale of ingenious proportion as to why he crossed the Gulf of Mexico to Havana, Cuba, with Charlie. Even I was impressed with his brilliant, off-the-cuff explanation.

With disgust on his face, Limbo stood up, stared eyeball to eyeball with Ramirez, and began his commentary.

"First of all, Ramirez, I am here on my own to try and help you. I do not like your tone or your condescending attitude. Now that I am here and see how you treat citizens who try and help you, I should have just told you to go fuck yourself when you asked me to meet you." As the sergeant tried to interrupt, Limbo held up his hand and continued, "Wait,

Ram-Her-Ez! I'm not finished," Limbo shouted.

I wanted to applaud and give a standing ovation for Limbo's unexpected performance but thought better. I just sat in my chair listening as did Sergeant Luis Ram-Her-Ez while Limbo continued.

"Not that I feel it is any of your business I'm gonna answer your question just so you can sleep tonight, Detective. Charlie Switzer was new to Key West, had a big new boat and seemed very nice at the time. He was somewhat of a novice on the water. I have thousands of hours spent in boats on the ocean. I was a local fishing guide for many years. When I joined Powell and Charlie on the fishing trip to the Tortugas, I guess Charlie was impressed with my fishing abilities. Or maybe he thought I had a nice ass. For all I know, Charlie could be gay. Who knows! But for whatever reason Charlie asked me to join him and fish our way to Cuba, have a few drinks in Havana and fish our way back to Key West. Why did he ask me? I have no idea. You'll have to ask him that question if you ever catch him. And frankly, Ram-Her-Ez, I hope you never do."

I could see the veins in Sergeant Ramirez's forehead pop out every time Limbo called him that. He was sweating so profusely his glowing red face seemed swollen enough to blow the top button off his starched uniform shirt. I was not only enjoying this moment, but I also appreciated the genius and motivation behind Limbo's tirade. He had completely disarmed Luis Ramirez. It was a brilliant maneuver that had the detective on the defensive.

As Limbo sat back down, I could not let his momentum die. I stood up and continued while answering the officer's last question, a question he left lingering in midair hoping somehow it would prove our connection with Hilda "the Hun" Tucker. I was calm, rational, and clear while I spoke, but I wanted to give him a little reprieve after Limbo's biting words cut him so deeply.

"Luis, could I please get a bottle of water now?" I asked.

He seemed almost relieved to get a moment to himself. As he walked out the door, he asked, "Dr. Adams, would you like something?"

Without looking up, Limbo shook his head no. When Luis reappeared with the water, I thanked him and noticed his color had returned to normal, and the swelling had started to subside. As he sat in his desk chair, I continued where Limbo left off.

"Luis, you asked why Hilda would deposit her entire life's savings in our two accounts. At first, we wondered the same thing, especially if she planned on a lawsuit against me for slipping in my store. We tried to contact her and ask her that very question, but as I am sure you know, Hilda had already disappeared. Her phones were disconnected, her clothes and furniture removed from her home, and there was no sign of Hilda Tucker anywhere."

"Well, how do you explain the money, Mr. Taylor?" Luis asked with a little more conviction in his voice.

"Luis! Really? Give us a little credit here. We do read the papers, and we are not stupid. I am sure we both know how that money got into our bank accounts. Hilda was already dead by then. You know it, I know it, and Limbo knows it. In fact, anyone who reads the *Key West Times* knows it. They found her severed nub that you identified from her fingerprint match in some fish," I said.

"Well, how did the money get from her account to yours and why?" Luis Ramirez asked.

"We both know how it got there, Detective. You know all about the fingerprint scanners at the bank and you know we all had accounts there. You also know by now that Charlie Switzer was on the bank's board. So I guess you just want to hear me say it. Okay, I will. Charlie Switzer must have killed Hilda, removed her thumb, and used it to access her banking accounts. We can all agree on that. Am I right, Luis?" I asked.

With a slight smirk on his face, he nodded yes.

So I continued. "I also know what you are thinking, Sergeant. The same question that has haunted Limbo and me ever since we noticed the deposit in our accounts. Why? Why would Charlie Switzer give us the money?"

"Exactly my point, Mr. Taylor, why? Was it a payoff? Was he buying your silence? Where is he?" Ramirez asked as he stood.

"Wait just a second there, Ram-Her-Ez," Limbo said as he stood back up. The sergeant sank back into his chair again.

"It was not any kind of payoff to hush us up or to buy our silence. We didn't know anything about this until we read it in the paper. So that kills your lame theory. All we could think of at the time was that he was trying to buy our friendship. But we never heard back from him. He never has contacted us, and we have no idea where he is. So that makes no sense either. The final conclusion we were able to come up with is that Charlie Switzer was setting us up. He was trying to pin her murder on Powell and me," Limbo said as he sat back down.

"Well, I know for a fact that you did not murder Hilda Tucker. All of the evidence points directly and exclusively to Charlie Switzer. We know he murdered the woman. We just don't know why. The only questions I have, the last questions I'll ask, are very important. Think hard before you answer. Have you heard from Charlie Switzer at all? Have you received any mail or correspondence from him? I mean anything at all?" the determined detective asked.

This was the moment Limbo and I had dreaded. We knew Charlie was guilty of murdering Hilda Tucker. We knew he had done an evil thing. We knew because he sent us the video of Hilda singing goodbye, the video that at this moment was on the back floorboard of my car outside. I knew from his expressions what Limbo's answer would be. He disliked Sergeant Luis Ramirez so much that his hatred for the man would surely override his sense of morality and justice. But for me, it was not that simple. It was as if I was about to meet my demise. My entire life flashed before my eyes. All of those years growing up in a home where honesty, integrity, and accountability were a way of life. Twelve years of Catholic education taught me about morals, ethics and living an honorable life. But at this moment, looking across the desk at Luis Ramirez, all I could remember from my Catholicism days were the Fifth Commandment and the guilt those days bestowed upon this wayward altar boy. I knew right from wrong. As ghostly figures of my favorite nuns and priests flashed before my eyes, I felt a strong hug from my father and the warm embrace of my mother when I was still an innocent child. Then while kneeling in a dark confessional, I heard the creak of the wooden window slide open. The priest from my parochial years turned an ear to hear my list of petty sins. These thoughts disappeared as quickly as they had surfaced. Now I saw my favorite high school nun teaching the importance of family and friends. "Love your family and your friends. Forgive them, never hold grudges, love thy neighbor," Sister Consuela was saying.

I snapped out of my trance when I heard Sergeant Ramirez repeat, "Well, are you going to answer my question or not? Have either one of you heard from Charlie Switzer?"

I ignored Limbo's presence, and spoke directly to Luis's face immediately, not giving Limbo time to respond.

"No Luis, how many times do we have to tell you we have not seen or heard from Charlie Switzer at all."

While the detective confirmed the answer with Limbo, I was searching my soul hoping not to be guilt-ridden for eternity. I wondered how many Hail Mary's Monsignor Gallagher would have made me say for my penance today. He would say that breaking the Fifth Commandment, Thou Shall Not Kill, is a mortal sin. Today I hoped that protecting that killer was venial.

On the ride to drop Limbo off at his boat, not a word was spoken. I knew we did the wrong thing today. I would have to live with that. When I crossed the bridge to Shark Key, I tossed the video into the deep channel. I hoped that not ever seeing the film again would make it easier to forgive my friend Charlie Switzer. And I prayed that time would erase the guilt and ease the pain I was sure to feel. Not having a copy of Hilda's taped farewell song also guaranteed I would never be able to show its evidence to Sergeant Luis Ramirez.

I called Dawn from the car on the way home. The joy and happiness in her voice were a welcome and much-needed diversion.

"Hurry home, Powell, I miss you. I'm making us a nice dinner tonight. We can just relax on the sofa, and you can tell me all about your day. I hope it all went well. Love you!" Dawn said.

When I arrived, she greeted me at the door with a kiss, a glass of wine, and the day's mail.

After the day I had, my feelings were scattered all over the place. My emotions had me on the brink of tears. "I love you, Dawn," I whispered.

I barely heard her when she replied, "Love you too, Powell." My focus was on an insured package she handed me with the mail. There was no return address, it simply said: "From Hilda."

Also included in the stack of mail, on the very bottom beneath the solicitation pamphlets, campaign notices, marketing materials, and Home Depot ads was the latest edition of the *Key West Times*. And although it would be weeks before I connected the dots, the bold headline stuck out like a sore thumb, so to speak. By the time I would add it all up, it would be too late. Charlie Switzer will have gotten away with murder, and I will have finally realized his selfish motivation in killing the fat lady, Hilda Tucker. It all became clear, the mystery solved when I reread these headlines after the fact, MISSING FLORIDA INSURANCE AGENT SEYMOUR TUCKER COLLECTS MILLIONS AFTER EX-WIFE'S MURDER.

CHAPTER 30

Many weeks passed by before Detective Luis Ramirez finally accepted the fact that Limbo and I had nothing to do with Hilda's disappearance. His list of suspects changed daily. When Limbo and I were still on that list, the detective would call or show up unexpectedly each and every day. I began to think that Ramirez kept talking to us just to get a read from our response. He seemed to like bouncing his theories off of the two of us to get our opinions. Or maybe he thought he could catch us in an incriminating lie. It was not until he discovered that Hilda's ex-husband Seymour Tucker had collected on her life insurance policy that Limbo and I were no longer suspects. But there were no connections between Hilda and Seymour that could prove the ex-husband's guilt. As far as Detective Ramirez could tell there had been no contact at all between the two for more than three years. Even so, Ramirez could not understand why Seymour Tucker had a multi-million dollar life insurance policy on his ex-wife. During our last meeting, Detective Luis Ramirez finally came to the right conclusion, the answer, and the truth about the murder of Hilda the Hun. Limbo and I had known the truth for some while now but never let Ramirez even suspect we did. He told us he was convinced that Charlie Switzer killed Hilda Tucker and that Seymour Tucker profited from the death. From his very thorough investigation, he knew Hilda was dead.

"The fact that the insurance company paid off the policy to the beneficiary is also reason enough to believe she is dead," he said.

Ramirez's frustration finally got to him when he realized that Hilda Tucker and Charlie Switzer had both disappeared from the face of the earth. Without Charlie Switzer or Hilda's dead body, he knew he could never prove the connection to Hilda's ex-husband Seymour. He also knew this case would never be solved and would torment him for years. When Luis Ramirez confessed all of this to me, I sensed his severe disappointment and hopelessness. I almost felt bad for the detective. He had put so much time and effort into this case, and now he was at a dead end. I really did feel badly, but not enough to tell him how I knew Charlie was guilty. And not badly enough to tell him about the video Charlie had made of Hilda. Even if I had it, it would do no good now. The video of Hilda's farewell was at the bottom of Shark Channel at mile marker 11.5. There was much more evidence that I withheld from the disappointed detective. The insured package delivered to my home ten days ago "From Hilda" would be absolutely convincing.

Inside was a photo of a tan and seemingly very happy Charlie Switzer. Standing beside him was a topless, attractive young girl with her arm draped around Charlie's neck. With each of them holding a very tropical-looking fruity drink, the background of palm trees, ocean, and white beaches was unrecognizable. The young girl's Latino and Hispanic features made me think the photo was taken somewhere on the coast of Cuba. If so, I was sure Charlie would not still be there. He was too smart to send a photo of where he would be living. Had I thought for a moment that Detective Ramirez would actively pursue this case and continue to search for Charlie, I might hand over the photo. It would be a cruel thing to do knowing Ramirez would probably spend a good part of the life he has remaining searching every inch of Cuba. Besides, I came to respect and like Luis Ramirez. I wanted him to forget this case and get on with his life. I hoped he could enjoy his family and forget about Hilda Tucker and Charlie Switzer. One of the last things that Detective Ramirez told me was, "I'm dropping the case and moving on. Life's too short to waste on things we can't solve."

His decision was the right one. And so was mine. I was sure that keeping all of the evidence away from him was the right choice. His reasoning for abandoning Charlie's pursuit had convinced me.

"They found Charlie's boat floating offshore about forty miles southwest of Key Largo early this morning," Ramirez had told me.

When I asked if there was any sign of Charlie, he replied, "No. None. But the boat was covered in blood, Charlie's blood."

When I asked the obvious question, he explained that the puddles of O-negative blood that coated the deck of *Heads Up* did indeed match Charlie's blood type.

As happy as I was that Charlie's death provided closure for Detective Ramirez I knew better. I had the proof. The evidence, as Luis Ramirez would have called it, was a graphic video of Hilda's last moments and the contents of the insured package I received "From Hilda" today. Charlie Switzer was most definitely alive and well.

CHAPTER 31

Alton Curtis Pinder had spent the last five weeks carefully covering his tracks. After his hard-to-pursue trek around the Gulf of Mexico, he made a home on a small remote and secluded island between Mangrove Cay and South Andros in the Bahamas. With his dark tan from weeks in the sun, his new but convincing Bahamian dialect of the local language and his clever alias, he convinced himself and everyone around that he was a native Bahamian of European descent. Charlie spent several weeks studying the language on Google, visiting local conch shacks and hanging out with Bahamian fisherman. He soon realized native Bahamians don't pronounce all of the letters in De English alphabet. He seldom if ever heard dem use an H, T, G, or W. His best teachers were duh fisherman. Charlie loved hanging out with them and catching fish.

"Ey Alton-mon, duh chirren dem is cachin duh fishes."

After a day on the water, the fisherman asked Charlie, "Alton, how you cook dem snappa's?"

"I fry dem fishes in duh erl," he replied.

Early in his recent education, Charlie learned a critical new phrase. One afternoon he had run up to Mangrove Key to get some fritters at the conch shack. He was sitting on a stool at the wooden bar eating his fritters and drinking a cold Kalik. Minding his own business, he was listening attentively to the loud locals who be talkin' bout de tourist who come to Bonefish. The more they drank, the louder they got. Obviously fishing guides, they were all talking about one of the anglers from New Jersey. When the owner of the shack showed up behind the bar, one of the guides

139

said, "Ey Shine, today I fish wit a biggety mon. He bring two other men wit him. Dat boat vas jam up. He neva shut he mout up. When we get back to dock he not give me a tip. He not say nuttin. When he look at me, I give him one big cut eye."

Shine and the other guides all laughed and held up their beer bottles toasting the biggety mon.

Charlie felt relieved that afternoon. The fisherman had carried on the entire conversation in front of him as if he were one of them, just another local. Charlie realized that a biggety mon was a loud, obnoxious, unlikeable sort. He figured a boat that was "jam up" was over-crowded. But it was not until later that he found out that a "cut eye" was a look of hatred and contempt.

When Alton Pinder transferred all of his money from the Cayman Islands to his new bank in Nassau, he watched closely with everyone who assisted him with the large monetary transfer. He was happy to know that everything went smoothly and the bank staff was all friendly and very helpful. He felt assured no one suspected him of any wrongdoing and he did not see one "cut eye." As he was walking out of the bank, he overheard the attractive young teller say to her boss, "Dat mon, he gat plenty money."

Life was good for Alton Pinder. His plan had worked just as he knew it would. Charlie Switzer's new life as Alton Curtis Pinder gave him the lifestyle he had always dreamed of. He spent his days fishing and diving. Some mornings he would pole the flats in his new Bahamian skiff looking for a bonefish or permit to cast a fly to. Other days he might collect conch and lobster for dinner. If the wind was slight and the seas calm, he would navigate *Thumbs Up* offshore to search for wahoo, tuna, or dolphin. Or maybe, like today, he would just pull up a lounge chair to the water's edge under a palm tree, sip Bahamian beer, and daydream. He would often reminisce of where he had come from, how he made it here, and the turbulent journey in between. But Alton Pinder never would think about what Charlie Switzer had to do in exchange to get this luxurious lifestyle.

This morning before Alton Pinder found his way to the lounge chair, he and his latest girlfriend, Kiara, frolicked naked in the shallow water for hours. Kiara is twenty-three, very petite with a huge inviting smile.

Her smooth, perfect skin is stained a beautiful dark brown from years under the Caribbean sun. She has been living with Alton for a few weeks. They both enjoy each other's company, spending all their time together. And the sex is a big bonus for Alton. Charlie would sometimes laugh when he would read the confused look on Kiara's face if he forgot to speak with Alton's dialect. Their relationship is not serious. They both accept that fact and just decided to enjoy their time together. The realization that Alton is twice her age does not bother Kiara in the least. Besides everything else positive, they also laugh a lot. Alton has the same fun-loving, outgoing personality as Charlie Switzer did. Kiara would always break into uncontrollable laughter when Alton would play "their song." It had been a favorite of Charlie Switzer's for years. Her favorite line in Toby Keith's song, "Who's Your Daddy?" was when the country singer would say, "I got the money if you got the honey, let's cut a deal."

Kiara went inside to shower while Alton relaxed in his lounge chair. The small ocean waves lapped quietly at his feet when a most unusual memory popped into his head. He closed his eyes, leaned back in his chair and relived the only bad marketing idea he had ever delivered.

Before Charlie Switzer made his fortunes from the Pfizer Group and with his even more profitable secretive ventures, his early marketing ideas crashed and burned. A regional Florida-based airline had contacted Charlie's marketing company seeking help. The airline was losing money trying to compete with the bigger airlines like Delta and American. They began to charge a fee for each checked bag which enticed the traveler to carry on their bags and not check them. In a year's time, customer complaints were at an all-time high. The top concern for customers was that the seats were too small for larger-boned people. Next on the list was that frequent fliers would get pissed off if they checked their bags and they had to deal with all of the others who carried on everything they own then tried to stuff it all into the overhead bins and under everyone's seats. The biggest and most understandable complaint was from customers who had to pay an extra fifty dollars if their bag weighed over forty pounds.

When the airline contacted Charlie for his advice, they wanted to improve customer relations but mostly wanted to increase their profit.

After many hours of thought and preparation, along with his uncanny ability to convince his clients, the airline accepted Charlie Switzer's proposal and began a six-week trial period. Charlie's plan showed the importance of weight and balance on an airplane. His research taught him more about airplanes, flight, and weight and balance than most pilots knew. If a plane is overloaded, luggage is removed from the plane and sent on the next flight. This caused many problems and stressed out many unhappy customers. "You charged me fifty dollars extra for my bag, and now I have to wait until tomorrow to get it?" some would complain. Charlie realized it was not fair. Why should one person have to pay extra for a piece of luggage that weighed forty-one pounds while a woman who weighs three hundred and fifty pounds pays nothing if she has a carry-on? It took three weeks to install the large scales at every counter in Florida where the airline departed from. Customers could check one bag for free and a second bag for twenty-five dollars. The price of the ticket, however, was determined by the weight of the traveler with his carry-on bag. With the exception of the first class, everyone was charged by the pound. Charlie's formula was quite simple. Take the old cost of the ticket and divide it by one hundred and fifty for women and two hundred for men. That gives you a per pound price. So for instance, if the flight from Tallahassee to Miami was four hundred and fifty dollars, a woman would pay three dollars per pound, and a man would pay two dollars and twenty-five cents per pound. A woman who weighed one hundred and ten pounds would pay three hundred and thirty dollars for a ticket. But the lady that weighs in at three hundred and thirty-nine pounds would fork out over a thousand dollars for her ticket. Charlie and the entire management group for the regional airline were all terminated on the same day, the last day his plan was implemented. It was also the same day the airline filed bankruptcy.

Charlie was abruptly awakened from his recurring nightmare when his disposable cell phone rang.

Alton Pinder answered, "Yeh mon, Ello. Who dis?"

"Charlie, it's Seymour. I have another job for you," the voice said.

"I'm retired, not interested," Charlie answered as he was about to toss the phone into the ocean.

"Wait!" the man said. "This one will be a piece of cake compared to Hilda."

Charlie decided to hear him out.

"You still there, Charlie?" Seymour asked.

"Yeah, go ahead. I'm listening."

Seymour Tucker explained to Charlie that his next target was an attorney by the name of Simon Morton of The Morton and Morton Law Firm in Sarasota.

"He's suing the hell out of most of the insurance companies I represent. Like I told you before, slip-and-fall lawsuits like Hilda's are more common than ever. Mr. Morton is living a lifestyle of the rich and famous because of it."

As Charlie listened to Seymour Tucker, he was very tempted, especially when he learned that the job paid two and a half million dollars. After briefly weighing the risks against the huge payday Charlie did something he never was able to do before. He declined. Charlie knew he had already used up eight of his nine lives. He would save the last one to enjoy life and the rewards those earlier eight lives of greed provided. While Seymour Tucker spoke into the phone trying to convince Charlie otherwise, a memory from his childhood came back to him.

His dad used to play a weekly game of poker with a few of his friends. Occasionally Charlie's dad would have to bring him along for whatever reasons. On one of those visits, he watched his dad closely as he piled up his large stack of chips. But before they left that night, his father had not only lost all of the winnings, he lost an additional ten thousand dollars. Charlie felt very sad when he saw his dad near tears and wondered why he didn't quit when he was so far ahead. An older man, a man named Abe Levin who had won big that night saw the sadness and despair in Charlie's eyes. Mr. Abe leaned over, handed Charlie an envelope with the ten thousand dollars to give back to his father and said, "Remember son, get greedy, become needy."

"Hello! Hello? You there, Charlie?" Seymour yelled.

"I'm here, but I'm not interested. I've retired Mr. Tucker, please do not ever try to contact me again or I may come out of retirement for one last job," Charlie said as he tossed the phone towards the water.

Charlie had a distinct advantage over Seymour Tucker, the only witness who really knew the truth. He knew where Seymour lived, worked, and played, a luxury that Mr. Tucker did not share.

Charlie had finally cashed in his chips. He quit while he was ahead. Alton Pinder hoped Charlie Switzer could resist the desire for wealth and the temptation to leave the Bahamas to visit the Keys. If not, Charlie would surely be caught. Making contact with his friends or giving in to the only one of the seven deadly sins that plagued him would be his downfall.

Kiara's timing was perfectly planned as she handed Charlie a cold beer and laid down beside him on his chair. Alton Pinder kissed Kiara lightly on the lips, smiled and told her how happy he be.

CHAPTER 32

I immediately recognized the green suede ring box stuffed in the bottom of the insured package addressed to me "From Hilda." However, when I opened it up, I was overwhelmed with its contents. I felt a tear trickle down my cheek when I read the attached note. On the back of a Southernmost Sea Burial pamphlet was written, "Powell, my friend, I wish you and Dawn a lifetime of adventure, love, and happiness. This ring was meant to be on Dawn's finger. Love you both, Charlie."

I could not believe what I was seeing. Charlie Switzer just gave me the eight-carat emerald-cut diamond that he paid almost nine hundred thousand dollars for. I was so touched and surprised. I looked at the note again to reread it when I noticed the P.S. at the bottom. It read, "P.S. Check box thoroughly. There is a package for you too, Powell. C.S."

I could not imagine what else Charlie would possibly have sent me. Fingering through the packing, I found it. It was a sample package of twenty-five blue pills from the Pfizer Corporation. I laughed out loud knowing Charlie would have loved to have seen my reaction when I opened the bag of Viagra. Well, that did it. I had already been thinking about popping the question soon. I had no reasons not to now. I'd never felt so in love with anyone. I had an incredibly expensive and rare diamond engagement ring and enough Viagra to keep my pecker hard for months. That thought made me laugh out loud again.

I was pretty sure Dawn and I had never discussed the fact that Charlie had purchased an engagement ring from me. At least I hoped not because I decided to propose this coming Saturday night with the ring. I want it to be the perfect proposal, a romantic date night and a memorable evening. After going back and forth trying to decide between hitting a knee on Sunset Key or on Little Palm Island, I settled on the latter. I booked a room on the island for Saturday night and reserved a table on the beach at sunset. This would be the most romantic and meaningful night of our lives. I ordered a tropical floral arrangement for our thatched bungalow and roses for the dinner table. Working with the amazingly competent and friendly resort staff, I quickly understood why Little Palm Island was the number one destination for the rich and famous. From the moment we would arrive at the docks, the precise attention to every minute detail was planned to be impeccable. From relaxing spa services, diving and fishing charters to romantic wedding packages this magical island promises a paradise that we all dream of. The lush island's concierge services also included their very own priest, rabbi, or minister of choice complete with everything you'll need to get a marriage license. Hopeful for a yes from Dawn, this was one amenity I hoped to take advantage of Saturday night.

Dawn did not suspect anything out of the ordinary when I told her date night this week was on Little Palm. We occasionally would go out there for dinner. I was so excited and nervous I could hardly wait until Saturday night. Friday, the day before the big night, I pulled the ring from its hiding place. When I did, the package of Viagra fell out on the floor. At thirty years old, I never had any need for the blue pill, but I began to wonder just what it did. I had seen the television advertisements that warned about the possibility of a four-hour erection. I then thought about going back to that romantic bungalow on Little Palm Island, after a bottle of good wine and an eight-carat diamond engagement ring on Dawn's finger. How nice would it be to have sex for four hours? But what if it had the opposite effect? I'd be sitting there in paranoia on Little Palm Island with a nice wine buzz, a horny fiancée, and a limp dick in my hand. Then it hit me. I better do a trial run, take a practice pill. Since tomorrow was the night for the proposal, it had to be tonight. Right after dinner as we sipped a glass of twenty-year tawny port, I swallowed one of the blue pills when Dawn wasn't looking. For the first ten minutes, I sat there waiting for my penis to jump out of my pants. It didn't happen. After about twenty minutes, my head felt like it was going to implode. I sipped some more port. Next, I felt a bit dizzy and like I might throw up. I didn't move. I did not want Dawn to notice any strange behavior. I drank more port. Finally, I could not take it anymore, my nose was running, I felt like I had a fever and I was pretty sure my balls were on fire. I tried to stand up and go to the restroom without alarming Dawn. When I stood, my vision was so blurred I didn't notice that my penis felt like it was the size of a fire hose until I ran into the television. I finally managed to close the door behind me in the bathroom. When I looked in the mirror, my entire face was the color of a bad sunburn, and small drops of blood dripped from my nose. My eyes were beyond bloodshot and bulging out of their sockets, and when I tried to urinate I checked the toilet closely for the bloody pins and needles, I was sure were coming from my enlarged member. When I looked down to locate the pain, I then noticed that my testicles were the size of grapefruits, and if I weren't mistaken, they were covered in a gnarly rash that resembled the hide of an armadillo. I stuffed myself back into my pants, zipped them up as far as possible then ran out to retrieve the bag of Viagra. I returned to the toilet and flushed the remaining twenty-four pills. When I returned to my chair, I could read the concern on Dawn's face. Before she asked, "I'm okay, just have an upset stomach," I told her while hiding my lap with pillows. Luckily when I woke up the next morning, I was completely back to normal. Tonight would be a great night. Thank God above I tried that pill last night instead of tonight.

The Truman, a beautiful old wooden boat, was the water taxi that ferried us from Torch Key to Little Palm Island. As Captain Ron maneuvered the boat through the shallow waters, I asked him if the island would be crowded tonight.

"Not too bad. I brought a family of four and two other couples out earlier, so I believe it will be a quiet evening." Captain Ron replied.

"Are they locals?" I asked.

"No, the family is from Miami, down for a week. One couple is from Sarasota celebrating their fiftieth wedding anniversary, and the other couple came by boat from the Bahamas," Ron said as we pulled up to the dock.

I thanked Captain Ron for the ride, took Dawn's hand, and walked her to the stern of *The Truman*. As we were about to disembark I looked around, taking in the beauty that surrounded us.

"This might be one of the most gorgeous places on earth," I told Dawn.

Of all the times I have visited Little Palm Island, its lush environmentally friendly surroundings are always breathtaking. As with past visits, I expected Tattoo to run out of the dock, point to the sky and yell, "De plane, De plane!" Exploring Fantasy Island tonight with my fiancée should be excitingly romantic and hopefully very amorous, especially after I put that diamond ring on her finger. The butterflies flying around in my stomach were not from the anticipation of asking Dawn to marry me, they were from the big surprise I had planned for later. The world-class concierge on the island took care of every detail with meticulous perfection. Our beachside table for two, inches away from the water's edge, was set with candles, pink hibiscus, palm fronds, and a slightly chilled bottle of French Bordeaux. As we enjoyed a fabulous meal of coconut lobster bisque, pan-fried yellowtail snapper, and asparagus gratin, our own private violinist serenaded us with the most romantic music. With her pants rolled up, standing ankle deep in the ocean, she splashed water on a pair of Key deer when they grabbed a hibiscus from our table. The two tiny deer pranced off into the dark. When we finished our desserts, the chef appeared beside our table right on cue. With the violin music playing, I stood and faced Dawn, nodded to the chef, and went to one knee. Dawn was so ecstatic and caught up in the moment that she did not see the chef's camera.

"I cannot imagine a better setting in the world than here, and I cannot imagine living my life without you. Dawn Landry, will you be my wife?" I said as I opened the ring box.

"Powell, Powell oh my god! Yes! Yes! Yes! Of course, I will. I love you!" she replied.

When I placed the ring on her finger her eyes lit up, and she knelt down in the sand beside me, kissing me while wiping her tears on my sleeve.

"Oh Powell, I am the happiest girl in the world, I wish we could get married tonight," Dawn whispered.

Although the chef's camera was constantly flashing, I was able to catch his eye and give a quick wink. I pulled Dawn to her feet and said, "I was hoping you would feel that way because I want to marry you tonight, too."

With the surprised look on Dawn's face lit up by the moon's light, it was the most beautiful I had ever seen her. The chef had slipped away and returned with Father O'Hara from Saint Peter's Catholic Church up on Big Pine Key. The friendly priest was so prepared, he had obviously rehearsed the ceremony as if knowing Dawn would say yes. The way he called us by our first names with such ease felt natural. After he pronounced us husband and wife, we hugged our newly formed wedding party goodbye and walked the beach back to our room hand in hand.

When we opened the door to our private bungalow, it was just as the brochure had promised. What awaited us was a richly romantic scene with the soft glow of candlelight illuminating the chilled bottle of champagne and chocolate-covered strawberries. The island gods had also drawn a decadent hot bath for Dawn and me that was infused and perfumed with bath salts and rose petals. It was a perfect romantic honeymoon evening, and I did just fine without Charlie Switzer's twenty-five pill gift pack. It was long after midnight when Dawn and I were relaxed enough to fall asleep. It had been a very full day.

Wrapped up tight in Dawn's arms before dozing off I listened to the rhythm of the tree frogs under the glow of the stars as the brochure guaranteed. All I heard was some blaring country music creeping into our love nest through the thatched cottage walls. When I stuck my head out the door, I soon concluded that the country twang emerged from offshore. The fronds from huge coconut palm trees blocked the moon's light making it impossible to see the source. When I slipped back under the silk sheets, Dawn asked, "Is everything okay? Where's that music coming from?"

"Yeah, everything is fine. It's just some redneck insomniac with a boat and a fondness for Toby Keith," I said.

"I like Toby Keith's music," Dawn replied.

"I know, try to get some sleep. Love you."

The music stopped at exactly ten after four in the morning. Dawn let me sleep until ten before she woke me with a kiss and a cup of coffee.

The boat was gone.

EPILOGUE

The years floated by with clear purpose flowing in a gradual current that crept slowly but steadily like a continental drift. The friendship and love that Powell Taylor and Dawn Landry felt for each other grew stronger each day.

In the days that passed since the horrible murder of Hilda Tucker, Charlie Switzer was able to put it all behind him as if it never happened. He had finally settled down and was able to enjoy life. Charlie's need for greed was part of the past. But his hopes to return to his previous life, knowing it was impossible, sometimes preyed upon him late at night. After three years, by day he and Kiara danced on the shore together with no worries. By night he prayed to a god he never knew pleading for absolution. It was in darkness when Charlie most missed his family and friends that he left behind. Luckily, daylight stripped away the fear and sorrow that came in the late hours after sunset. Knowing there was a risk of being discovered, Charlie still sent photographs occasionally to Powell, Dawn, and Limbo. It is the only connection he still had left to his past. The hopes that they will all get together again somehow was a recurring thought on many of those long sleepless nights. Charlie and Kiara had a good life and a great future. Living on an island in paradise suited them both. They fished, they dove, they collected conchs, and they loved life. And they still laugh. Kiara likes the money and Charlie loves the honey.

After the wedding, Powell sold Caribbean Jewelers to Devin and her girlfriend, Candace. He worked out a deal where he kept the building and let them lease the space and pay him monthly for the business. Devin finally cleaned up her language and successfully ran the jewelry store. She was able to double the monthly payments after the first year and would have Powell paid off in seven short years.

Powell and Dawn decided to take advantage of the valuable real estate above the jewelry store. Since it faced Duval Street, the space was in great demand. Duval Street is the most visited tourist destination in all of Florida. It is Key West's main street and stretches from the Atlantic Ocean to the Gulf of Mexico. This historical street which was named after the first territorial governor of Florida is just over one and a quarter miles in length. The ambitious tourists who do the Duval Crawl will walk past many interesting sites between Mallory Square and the southernmost point of the United States. The carnival-like atmosphere never ends. Pedi-cabs, mopeds, bikes, trolleys, and the popular conch train are constant travelers on this crowded street. The attractive force that draws thousands of people daily includes the Cuban influence seen in cigar stores and the restaurants with phenomenal Cuban cuisine. Besides being a great place to shop for art, trinkets, t-shirts, and souvenirs, the street is alive with bars, outdoor cafés, and music. Many famous bars and bodegas that add to the colorful cultural influence of this seaside town include Sloppy Joes, Margaritaville, Captain Tony's, The Bull and Whistle, and Rick's Café. Right in the middle of the ever-so-profitable, popular and thriving street proudly stands Caribbean Jewelry.

After considerable thought, many conversations with savvy retailers and several different scenarios, Powell and Dawn decided on the best use for the space above the jewelry store. They built an apartment for themselves in the northern half of the upstairs and leased the southern half to Baby's Coffee Shop. Powell had originally wanted the tenant to be a well-known, highly recognizable coffee shop chain. But in the weeks before the renovation started, that coffee giant he had negotiated with decided to get political and take a controversial stand on hiring refugees. Powell had remembered what his father taught him at an early age.

"In business, never get political, Powell. No matter what side you take, you're gonna always piss off half of your customers."

Powell wanted income, not controversy. Besides, Powell and

Dawn both liked Baby's coffee better. It was all freshly roasted locally at mile marker 15.

The spacious New Orleans-style balcony that faced west and over-looked Duval Street was shared. Baby's had tables and chairs for customers to enjoy. Dawn had decorated their space with plants, outdoor furniture, and a barbecue grill. The couple's favorite nights to spend at the Duval apartment were during the holidays. They would grab a bottle of wine and watch the street party until long after the bars had closed. Their two favorite times of the year were Fantasy Fest in October and New Year's Eve. Friends and family always showed up to enjoy these two festivities. During Fantasy Fest it was the thousands of tourists who showed up wearing only body paint that amused Powell the most.

"Wow. Some of those people really need to put some clothes on," he would say.

It was New Year's Eve that was always Dawn's favorite time. Di-rectly across the street from their apartment was the Bourbon Street Pub. Thousands of visitors packed the street hours before midnight to enjoy the live entertainment that featured the men of Bourbon. Down the street at midnight, Sloppy Joe's had the Conch Drop, Schooners has the Wench Drop, but across the street from Caribbean Jewelers, The Bourbon Street Pub dropped Sushi, the Drag Queen in the Red Slipper. It was always a hit with whoever showed up on the balcony that night.

With their home on Cudjoe Key and the apartment on Duval Street, there was always plenty of room for Powell and Dawn's family and friends to visit.

It was a good life, a life in the Keys that both enjoyed. Powell and Dawn seldom talked about the past. Those memories brought sadness, regret, and guilt. Instead, they lived each day like newlyweds, inseparable while enjoying every moment they had together, making up for lost time. They spent their days mostly on the water—fishing, snorkeling, picnick-ing, and celebrating every sunset every night.

Captain Limbo was possibly the happiest of all. He donated his old wooden Schooner to Mel Fisher's Salvage Company to use as a display to welcome guests to their museum. It was the perfect believable prop for that business. It looked as if it had spent many decades underwater. With the large barnacles on her bottom along with the newly added pirate's flag and crow's nest with a freshly painted stern that read *Queen Anne's Revenge*, she could easily have passed for Blackbeard's sunken ship.

His new fifty-six-foot sailing yacht, as he liked to call it, was anchored in Cudjoe Bay. By the time he rigged it like he wanted, purchased new bed linens, towels and carpet and stocked the bar, Limbo had spent the majority of the one hundred sixty-three thousand dollars his friend Charlie Switzer had donated. The remaining moneys were used to refinish, varnish, and paint his old Ford station wagon. Woodie had not looked this good since it rolled off of the assembly line in 1950. For the first time since Limbo had received the car from his uncle as a gift, Woodie's air conditioner, heater, and radio were now all in perfect working condition.

Every Sunday afternoon for the past year and a half, Powell and Dawn had a cookout on their dock behind their Cudjoe home. The invitation list always included a few friends and any family members who might be visiting. Limbo showed up early every Sunday aboard his new dinghy sporting his white linen pants, a short sleeve black linen Guayabera shirt, and bare feet. And always, every week, he arrived with a gorgeous girl on his arm. But seldom was it the same woman two weeks in a row. Today's Sunday outing would be no different. Limbo and Raven idled up the canal and tied a line to the dock about four o'clock. Limbo introduced Raven to Powell and Dawn, grabbed a beer from the ice chest and asked Raven, "What you drinking, babe?"

"You got a slippery nipple?" she asked.

"I don't think so," Limbo and Powell answered in unison. Powell looked at Limbo with one raised eye brow as to say, WTF? Raven decided on some white wine for her second choice of beverage.

"What's to eat, guys?" Limbo asked while trying to lighten the mood. Dawn had made a West Indies crab salad and a key lime pie for desert. Powell was cooking a back home Gulf Coast favorite that his dad used to do on their dock on Pensacola Bay.

"In South Carolina, they call it a low country shrimp boil," Powell explained.

In a big pot of boiling water with cut-up lemons, onions, salt, pepper, and liquid crab boil, Powell added potatoes, sausage, corn, and shrimp. He told Raven he would then dump it all in the middle of the picnic table on newspaper right before sunset. She tried to smile.

"Raven, do you live in Key West? What do you do there?" Dawn asked.

"Oh, yes. I'm a dancer," she replied.

There was an awkward pause before Limbo finally said, "Powell, I'm starving. Can we crank up that shrimp boil yet?"

After dinner the four of them sat around sipping their wine looking out over Cudjoe Bay.

"Limbo, how did you decide to set anchor in Cudjoe Bay? There are hundreds of miles along the Keys that are beautiful," Powell asked.

Limbo told the group it was because it was a safe harbor protected from most winds, it had deep water and easy access to the ocean. But then he explained the real reasons.

"I can park Woodie in your driveway, I am only a few minutes away from Sunday dinner, and I've gotten accustomed to the smell of monkey shit that comes with a south wind."

"I was wondering what that odor was. I was hoping it wasn't one of you," Raven said.

With just enough light to see across the bay, Limbo pointed and said, "Look, Powell, there's a boat anchored up next to my sailboat."

"I see it, Limbo. That has to be the biggest center console boat I've ever seen," Powell answered.

The "shit wind" as Limbo had named it was south-southeast tonight. From where they sat they could easily read the boat names stenciled on the sterns of the two boats.

"Why is your boat called *Ram-Her-Ez*? Is it a sexual thing?" Raven asked Limbo.

Limbo started to explain but finally just said, "It's a long story. I'll explain later."

Limbo lied. Raven would never hear the story, and she would not be back for dinner next Sunday. Powell was really impressed with the size of the boat anchored next to Limbo's.

"I'd like to get a closer look at that center console out there if it's still there tomorrow. Can you make out the name Limbo?" Powell asked.

Only moments ago the sun had disappeared, and the refracted pink light made the stern of the boat difficult to see.

Limbo squinted hard changing the shape of his eye, allowing what little light that was left to be focused better while decreasing the amount of light entering his eye. Excited that it had worked Limbo exclaimed, "Yes! Yeah, I can see it. It's *Thumbs Up!*"